Blood Rites

Dead Rites Series, Volume 2

Markus Danielson

Published by Markus Danielson, 2024.

BLOOD RITES

First edition. October 31, 2024.

ISBN: 979-8227990426

Written by Markus Danielson.

This book is dedicated to my three angels in heaven—my Mom Alice, my friend Rachel, and my dog Gizmo. I miss and love you all.

In addition, this book is also dedicated to my dad, my sister, my brother, my brother-in-law, my sister-in-law, my best friends my family, and my goddaughter.

Dead Rites Part 2 Blood Rites
By
Markus Danielson
There's something in the blood...
It runs in the blood...
The blood is tainted...

There are only two kinds of vampires.
Hunters: Good Ones
And Dead Ones
Laurell Hamilton

Prologue

I have been doing this for ninety years. Ninety fucking years. These Dhampir eyes and body have seen it all and done it all. I died in 1935 but was reborn on Halloween. Since then, I have been on a mission. Since I killed Bonnie and Clyde, the Invictus Society has me killing vampires while I look for the six Gods of Vampires. I have found out later on that there is an unidentified seventh God of Vampire. Let me give you a quick history. April 30th, 1945, I killed that little German bastard and his henchmen. His girlfriend killed herself before I got the chance to do her. On the same date, April 30th, but in 1975, I killed one of the seven Gods. Then again in 1986 I killed the second God of vampire. Thank goodness I had help with that son of a bitch. The other God of vampires were easy to find and kill.

The Invictus Society tells me what to do. They have had me doing several different missions here and there.

My sister Val long ago retired. She met a good guy named Joey, whom she decided to settle down with and marry. He was good to her. They both stayed in New York to run her bar till her passing in 1960 and then him a few months later. They didn't have any kids.

As for my wife Rebecca, we did stay together, even with what I became. But in 1970 she passed away from cancer. I laid her to rest alongside mine and Leah's graves.

My daughter Leah is still in a comatose state. She is all grown up but looks like she is twenty-one. In reality, she should be ninety-five. I wish she would wake up. I look forward to the day that she does.

The mega bitch, Akasha, is still a stone giant. The Invictus Society has her locked up in a hidden area. They have certain people who just sit there and watch her big clump of stone around the clock. They didn't want to take any chances of her psychotic followers trying to free her.

Pilar is still breathing for now. She is locked up along with other followers of Akasha's. I have visited her a few times. I miss the person she used to be. She sounds like a crazy person.

"My Akasha master will wake up from her slumber and you will all be fucked," is all she will ever say. We have tried to feed her, but she refuses to eat. I've seen her eat a few bugs. It was disgusting but hey, at least she is eating something. The Invictus Society wanted to behead her, but I requested to keep her alive. I hoped one day we would discover a cure. In reality, she is all I had left besides Leah.

As for me, since I've became a Dhampir vampire hunter, I have gained new abilities over the years. Also, some weaknesses as well. I feel young and look young, but I am 125 years old. I heal fast and I am immune to a lot of things like sickness and diseases and even religious stuff. I can go to church and not even be hurt by the church or even the crosses. I have been called, 'Day Walker' because the sun doesn't hurt me. I can eat regular food, I can hear and see from far away, and I even have a great memory. I have gained strength, speed, and agility, along with reflexes, stamina, sense aura, and my favorite, hypnosis. So, if I'm in a bad mood I can just hypnotize a random person and make them do stupid shit but not too much. I don't want them to go to jail, I did have a wolf companion with me for a while. I named him Ace.

Unfortunately, we had to take a break in 2020 due to the Corona Virus. We had to quarantine the entire state of New York and the world, but we are back in business. I have killed three out the seven Gods within the last few decades.

Now I'm here in the year 2025, on this chilly October day with two of my bosses, April and Gina. They handed me an envelope with the whereabouts of the next vampire Gods. They keep telling me, *"Get the job done or we will pull the plug on Leah, and we will kill you. We know your weakness."* I just gave them a smug look as I took the envelope from April's hand to open it up. It was a picture of the next vampire, Klaus. Inside the envelope was his current location, where he lived, and what he was up to.

Apparently, him, Koi, and Rebekah are making and selling a drug called Vampir or V. According to the file, it turns regular people into vampires. It says people shoot them in their eyeballs and it takes effect quickly. It hasn't hit the States yet, just in Europe. Looks like I'm taking the private jet to England to look for these three vampires. I just hope I can save some people.

I gather my weapons and pause for a minute to look at my family picture from back in '35. Me, Rebecca, and Leah. I grinned remembering the good times. I hop into my 1971 Pontiac GTO and click the garage door clicker to open the garage. I headed out to LaGuardia Airport for a seven-hour flight to Heathrow. On the way to the airport, I had to think and clear my head. I wish I had a bottle of Jack and a cigar to go with it.

Chapter One

October 5th, 2025, 10:00 p.m., Daniel Benson checked his weapons after the plane landed at Heathrow Airport. He grabbed his bags and weapons before exiting the plane. Benson was met by his driver, who works for the Invictus Society, waiting on the runway for him.

"Mr. Benson?" The driver asked. He was wearing a black suit with a white dress button up shirt underneath, along with a black tie. The black cap he wore on his head matched his attire very well.

"Daniel Benson." He corrected the driver.

"My apologies. I'm Mr. Smith, your driver. I guess I'm taking you to your next mission." Smith announced to him. Smith had worked with the society for nearly a month now and he knows his way around London very well. Well, he should anyway. He was born and raised here.

Benson nodded his head and followed closely behind Smith as he led the way out of the airport and to his car. They walked up to a black BMW. Benson stopped to admire it. In all his years alive, he had never seen a car kept up. It wasn't a new BMW but it sure as hell looked better than any new vehicle on the market now-a-days. Smith opened the back trunk for

Benson to help him put his luggage in when Benson's phone began to ring.

"I'm here. I made it to London." Benson announced to the person on the end of the phone before climbing in the back seat of the car. He noticed the yellow file sitting in the empty seat next to him.

"You should have the file for your next mission. In the documents you will see where Klaus was last seen. Your hotel room has already been booked and ready for you." Noted the female voice on the other end. Daniel recognized it instantly. It was April.

Benson was about to hang up before April asked him to do a video chat with her, along with Gina and Robert, the weapons expert.

Benson accepted the invitation and within seconds all three of their faces were on one screen.

"Robert, these new weapons better work! I don't want them jammed up like last time." Daniel complained to Robert.

Robert Herrera, who served in the army as a former Captain, also fought in the Afghanistan and Iraq attacks. Aka the GWOT Global War on Terrorism. He was honorably discharged back in 2015. He even received the Purple Heart and Medal of Honor. The Invictus Society recruited him right after he retired.

"They won't, I double checked them myself. I'm excited about the new weapon I made. The rotary crossbow, all you have to do is hit the trigger once and arrows just keep flying out!" Herrera announced overly excited.

"And what about this Uzi nine-millimeter?" He asked Herrera.

"Ah yes, my favorite. The bullets are made with special silver, and it is blessed with a priest that I go to church with." Robert told him.

"Daniel how is your hunger doing? Have you been taking those blood pills to get over your cravings?" April interrupted them changing the subject.

"Yes, they work but I'm running low. When I come back, I'm going to need a refill from the doctor." Benson answered April.

"Benson, everything you need is in that folder. What Klaus looks like and the name of his club." Gina chimed in.

Daniel picked the folder on Klaus up and started going through the paperwork. He noticed two other vampire names in the file along with Klaus's.

"Question? Are Koi and Rebekah going to be at the club? If they are, this should be over and done within one take." He told them.

Before either one of them could answer, someone else joined in on the chat *"No, it won't be over till I say it's over."* The mysterious figure had a deep voice that Daniel didn't recognize.

"Who the hell are you?" Benson asked the figure.

"I'm April and Gina's boss. That means I'm your boss. I'm the one who gives you the orders. I'm the head boss for the Invictus Society and you do whatever I say and there won't be any problems. One mistake and I pull the plug on your daughter, and I will kill you! We know your weakness Daniel so don't fuck with Invictus Society! We brought you in and we can take you out." The deep voice figure told Daniel.

Benson grew angry. *"Well hello mister fancy pants. I've got news for you pal, you aren't leading anything but two things, jack, and shit. And jack left town."* Benson hissed at the figure.

"JUST DO YOUR GODDAMN JOB OR ELSE YOUR DAUGHTER GOES NIGHT NIGHT FOREVER AND YOU GO BYE-BYE!" The figure yelled at Daniel.

Daniel's phone screen went black. The figure must have ended the call. Daniel sat back and kept repeating in his head what the dark figure explained to him. He grew angry as his body started to heat up just thinking about it. Before he realized what he was doing, he felt his hand go through the window, busting it out. He quickly regretted it as the freezing air hit him. Daniel zipped up his leather jacket and folded his arms to try to keep warm. Smith looked at him through the mirror, but he kept silent. Luckily, they were almost at the hotel.

Daniel checked into his room and got into the elevator. He used his key to open the door. He wasn't surprised to see another boring room. The Invictus Society believed it to be low key, which meant Daniel never got to stay in the suites. Which he didn't mind at first but damn it was starting to get old. He unpacked his bags and checked his weapons. The good thing about private airplane customs is you don't have to check your bags. Benson was checking out his last weapon when he got a call on his cell phone. The caller was calling private. Which was weird because no one has his number. Only the Invictus Society. Daniel never answers private calls, but his former cop instincts told him to answer the phone.

"Hello?" Daniel asked suspiciously.

"Is this Daniel Benson?" asked the mysterious caller with a Russian accent.

"Yes, who are you? And how did you get this number?" Benson asked.

"Let's worry about names later. Will you meet me at the Royal Albert Dock in an hour? Come alone. I got a tip for you if you want to stop Klaus, Koi, and Rebekah." Stated the mysterious Russian man.

Before Benson could say anything else, he heard a click on the other end. The caller hung up. Benson looked at his watch, it was eleven thirty. He grabbed one of his guns and closed his hotel room door. He then hauled ass out of the hotel room to look for Smith. He had to convince Smith to give up the car key so he could go alone.

About an hour later, Benson finally found the docks where he was supposed to meet the unknown caller. Benson climbed out of the car and walked towards the gate. It was unlocked. Daniel went inside the docks and was surrounded by darkness. Only the moon would shine its light to help guide him. He walked all the way to the end of the docks before he was stopped by the voice he recognized on the phone. He couldn't see his face in the darkness. Only his dark figure.

"Daniel Benson." The Russian figure said his name.

"Yes, that's me. Mind telling me your name?" Benson asked, being cautious.

"Just call me 'Dock' since we are here at the docks. I know you're armed. Do you mind putting your gun down?" Dock asked Benson. *"I'm unarmed."*

Daniel debated whether he should put his gun down but eventually did what he was asked. *"Who are you? I can hear you but don't see you?"*

Dock came out from under the fog. He was wearing an old top hat with an old cape jacket. He dressed like he was from the 1700s. Once Dock opened his eyes Daniel noticed his eyes were glowing bright blue.

"What the hell? Are you a Dhampir too?" Benson asked amazed.

"Never mind that now." Dock rejected the question. *"You want your tip? Here it is. The Invictus Society is lying to you. Klaus is not here in London. He does live here, but his drug operation is in Moscow, Russia. Just under the St. Basil's Cathedral and his other operation is in Rome, France under the Vatican. You have forty-eight hours to destroy his shipment. The people here are turning fast, and I already had to kill some of them. You must not tell the Invictus Society."* Dock warned him.

"How do you know? And how do you know about the Invictus Society?" Benson wanted answers.

Dock threw something to Benson. It was the medallion that the Invictus Society wears. *"I was a former member; I knew your sister."* Dock told Benson.

Chills went down Daniels back when Dock told him that. He had more questions but before he could ask them, he heard a noise coming from behind him. He turned to look, and he saw some dock workers coming back from their break. Once he turned back to look at Dock he was gone. Only fog was left in his place. *"What the? So that's what it feels like!"* Benson noted to himself.

The voices were growing closer, so Daniel picked his gun up off the ground and hauled ass back to the car and returned to his hotel room.

After returning to the hotel, Daniel packed his bags and weapons and went to search for Mr. Smith to drive him to the airport. It was going to be a three-hour flight to Moscow.

Chapter Two

"Daniel, *do you mind telling us why you are not in London like we told you to?"* Gina was angry. So was April and the boss who all stared at him evilly on the video chat.

"I just got a hot tip that Klaus was in Moscow. I sense it, he is in Moscow. His operations were found there and in Rome. I know, trust me. If I'm wrong, then do what you need to do boss." He tried to explain.

"Alright, but if you're lying, we will not hesitate to kill you and your kid!" The Invictus Society boss threatened Daniel.

Daniel hung the phone up feeling upset once again about the threat the boss made toward his daughter. He felt it in his blood his source wasn't lying to him. The ringing of his phone broke his concentration. It was Robert calling.

"Yes Robert, what is it?" asked Daniel.

"Hey Benson, how's it going? How are the weapons working out for you?" Robert sounded eager.

"I don't know. I haven't tried them yet. Is this the reason you called me? To see if I used the new toys?" He asked him.

"No, the reason I'm calling is because I made some new bullets. These are wood bullets. The tips are made of wood, and they go with any of your guns. Two shots will just piss them off, but to kill them off, it will be three shots right in the heart. Not only

that, but I also made them for your shotgun as well. The pellets are made from the wood also and the pellets will blast their heads off!" Robert explained overly excitedly.

Benson smiled listening to how Robert talked about his new bullets. Robert had such confidence in his work. He liked that about Robert. If they got the job done and kept him alive then he would be happy.

"And yes, they are blessed by a priest so whenever you get back to New York they will be ready for you." He added.

"Well, I have never doubted you. You come up with the coolest weapons and other bang bangs." Benson chuckled.

"I'll see you when you get back." Robert told him before hanging up.

Benson's stomach started to cramp up and he was beginning to feel sick. He knew he was having cravings. This is what always happened when he had cravings. He reached into the pocket of his leather jacket and pulled out the bottle of blood pills. The Invictus Society's very own personal doctor gave them to him. It was a substitute for real blood. They didn't want him going around and draining people. Daniel took his normal dosage of two pills. It usually took him several hours before needing more.

The plane landed at Moscow airport. Once the plane's door opened, Benson noticed how quiet it was outside. After looking around with a puzzled expression, he confessed to himself, *"That's funny, the car should have been here."* He closed the airplane door and motioned the pilot to take off. He was then greeted by unexpected visitors. The Russian police. But they were all vampires.

"Hello comrades, (Friends) mind showing me around?" he asked sarcastically as he pulled out his crossbow and pointed it at them. They began hissing at him, and they all began to run towards him one by one. Benson started shooting them and they died with an instant shot.

"Yep, Dock wasn't kidding. Fuck! I need to go to the St. Basil's," Daniel told himself after he exterminated the vampires.

It was a cold Moscow night as Benson walked the streets trying to find transportation. He noticed an empty police car and climbed into it. The keys were still in the ignition. *"Please start,"* he told himself before turning the key. The engine roared. Daniel let out a sigh of relief. He headed in the direction of the Cathedral.

Russia just wasn't Russia anymore. As Benson drove through the city of Moscow he was in disbelief. Buildings were boarded up. There were fires all over the place. The city was covered with smoke. Cars were piled up in the streets. Either abandoned or left with dead bodies still in them. Bodies were everywhere. It looked like a horrific massacre took place.

Benson drove slowly down the streets until he came across something that made him hit his brakes. A vampire in the middle of the street sucking a human dry of his blood. The man was still jerking but Benson knew it was too late to save him. Benson gripped the steering wheel tightly and slammed his foot on the accelerator. The tires squealed as Benson pressed hard on the horn. The vampire looked up just in time for Benson to hit him. The vampire's head landed on the windshield of the police car.

"Sorry to ruin your dinner but you are one ugly motherfucker," Benson snickered to the head before turning on

the wipers and knocking the head off the car. *"Hundred points motherfuckers!"* He snickered being a wiseass again.

It took him a while to maneuver through the city, but he finally found the Cathedral and to his surprise it was guarded. *"Well, looks like these vampires are smart too."* He mentioned to himself. He climbed out of the car and grabbed his crossbow. He reloaded it and started to walk towards the Cathedral.

The vampire guards saw Benson and they started to hiss and run towards him. He pointed his crossbow at them and pulled the trigger, but something was wrong. The crossbow was jammed.

"GODDAMNIT ROBERT!" Benson shouted with anger. *"Looks like I'm doing this the old fashion way."* He said angrily.

He reached into the pockets of his leather jacket, and he grabbed some daggers. Daniel started slicing and dicing his way to the building. The vampire's body would evaporate with just a small stab in their hearts or heads. After he killed all the guards and seen that the coast was clear, Daniel put his daggers away and grabbed his custom-made Uzi, made with custom bullets that were made with silver tips blessed by the priest. If he shoots the vampires in the heart, they die quickly. And of course, he has his sword made with real silver in case he runs out of bullets.

Daniel approached the door and kicked it in. He pointed his weapon and started to scout the place. With him being a Dhampir, his eyesight was perfect. He can even see in the dark and see aura glow.

After scoping out the building, no vampires were in the Cathedral. Benson double checked the building with his aura sense, he saw something big in the basement. *"That has to be the lab."* he told himself.

Daniel stealthily walks to the basement with his gun still drawn. Not only focusing on the big thing in the basement, but also seeing if anything pops out at him. Once he reached downstairs, he turned on the light and he was instantly disgusted. Dead bodies everywhere. Some were drained and some were still hooked up to machines as their blood was being taken from them. It was a huge experiment lab down here. Daniel had to hold his nose due to the horrific smell of rotting decomposing bodies. Daniel kept his gun drawn in case something popped out at him. Once the coast was clear, he returned his gun back into the holster. He noticed a table with scattered paper in it. After getting a closer look, he realized they were notes for the experiments they were doing. Benson noticed something else. A note mentioning him. He grabbed the paper and read it.

We don't know who the day walker is. We don't know if it's a he or she. We do know that it is from New York. You must ensure secrecy. It must never know our plan. Our drug Vampir, must go on as scheduled. Soon we will free and wake up our queen mother Akasha and our God D...

The paper was covered with blood, *"Fuck!"* He muttered. *"I must take this for evidence."* He said out loud.

Just then Benson's phone rang. He grabbed it and looked at the caller ID. It was a private number.

"Dock?"

"I know you are at the Cathedral. Did you find what you need?"

"Yes, but no drugs. Just bodies."

"Never mind that, what I want you to do now, is blow up the building,"

"How? I don't have anything to blow it up with!"

"Look in the police car. We left you a gift."

"We?" Benson was puzzled.

"Yes, we. Now go! You are wasting time."

The phone went dead. So, Daniel gathered what he could of all the experiment papers and hurried up the stairs. He ran out of the Cathedral and to the police car. When he got there, there was a note on the windshield.

Leave the car. There is a motorbike around the corner. To blow up the Cathedral, look inside the trunk of the car.

He crumbled up the note after reading it and tossed it in the street and he popped the trunk of the police car. To his surprise, there was not one but two missile rockets. Benson just grinned. He took both missile rockets out of the car. He put one on the ground and took the other missile rocket and aimed it at the Cathedral. Once his aim was clear he shot it.

BOOM

The building goes up in flames, Benson gets the other rocket takes aim and again.

BOOM

Just to double check after that he felt a little weak from the fire, but he made it around the corner to see a very nice 2025 Harley Davidson Nightster motorcycle. Daniel hauled ass out of there as the sun was beginning to rise, he notices a few vampires beginning to burn up because of the sun he had to stop quick to see the vampires burn. He just shook his head in disgust as he put his sunglasses on and went to find a hotel to sleep it off.

Daniel finally found a hotel to sleep in for a few hours. When he came too, it was midafternoon. He decided it was time to get up and move around. He barely climbed out of bed when he got a phone call. He checked his phone's caller ID, and it was Smith.

"Benson it's me I'm outside waiting for you to take you to the airport the private jet is ready to go to Rome, Italy." Smith told Daniel.

"Be right down and watch your ass!" Benson told Smith before hanging up the phone.

Daniel's phone rang again instantly; he checked it, but this time it was Dock.

"Yeah?"

"Are you leaving Moscow to leave for Rome?"

"Yes, I'm leaving the hotel now. I know it's midafternoon, but I'll be there tonight to scope and see anything suspicious,"

"Good. Klaus should be there with his drugs, as well as Koi and Rebekah."

"I know, just make sure you leave me some rocket launchers or some dynamite or something so I can blow up everything."

Dock hangs up without replying. Daniel finished getting ready.

Daniel opened his hotel door and looked out of the hall; it was empty. So, he grabbed his bags and shut the door. He was hiding his weapons in his bag, the only gun he had out was hidden behind his back with his black leather jacket covering it. Daniel waited patiently for the elevator doors to open. Once they did, he noticed a woman already standing in the elevator. She was so breathtaking it made him nervous. He walked in the elevator and waited for the doors to close. He gave the woman a nervous smile and she returned one just the same. He glanced at her hoping not to be so obvious. Blonde hair, long legs, beautiful ocean blue eyes. In her early twenties.

"Kakoy etazh lifta?" (which elevator floor) She asked in a soft voice.

Benson smiled and replied, *"Vestibyul' otelya."* (hotel lobby)

She gently pushed the button, and he thought to himself, *"Man, how did I know what to say? How did I know what she said? This always amazes me."* One of the many powers Benson has been to speak several different languages. He never had to study them or anything. He could walk up to someone, and they could talk to him in a foreign language, and he knows what they said to him, and he knows what to reply to them.

They both stood side by side and being very quiet. Benson looked the woman up and down again. She was a beautiful sight. He noticed how jittery she was. He hadn't noticed it before. He thought she had too much coffee or energy drinks today. Out of nowhere she fell on the floor and her body went into convulsions like she was having seizures. She was faced down when she finally stopped moving. Daniel bent down on one knee to check on her. He turned her body around so he could see her face. To his horror, the Russian lady turned into a vampire. Benson jumped up from his knees and reached behind his back to grab his gun, but she was quicker, she picked up Daniel and slammed his body onto the elevator walls and the ceiling and floor making the elevator stop. Benson was on the ground when the woman climbed on top of him, showing her fangs and her big glowing red and yellow eyes. Daniel struggled to get her off him, but she had him pinned down. Her long slimy tongue licked the side of Daniel's face.

"Get off me you nasty bitch!" He exclaimed in disgust.

She leaned in closer towards him and sniffed him. *"BODRSTVUYUSHCHIY!"* (Day walker) she screamed. She lifted her left hand, revealing her claws. Before she could attack him, Daniel grabbed her hand with his free hand. She wrestled with him, and he was able to get his other arm freed. With all his strength, Daniel was able to overpower her and now he was on top of her. He reached for his gun and placed it on her forehead.

"DASVIDANIYA BITCH!" (goodbye)

BANG

Her body went limp. He got up and her body began to dissolve into ashes.

"That went well." He announced out loud.

Benson pushed the button for the lobby, and he noticed her purse on the ground. Being curious, he picked it up and rumbled through it. He found some paper and a wallet. He dug a little more and found a pair of her panties. He debated whether he should keep them. For evidence of course. Something shiny caught his eye. He grabbed the odd object and dropped the purse to the floor. It was an eye drop case with the letter V on it.

"Son of a bitch! They are injecting it into their eyeballs. I wonder how long it takes to turn them into these damn vampires?" Daniel wondered.

Before the elevator could stop, Daniel scattered the ashes around to make it look like it was just dirt on the floor. He grabbed the purse and her shoes off the floor and stuffed them in his jacket, hoping it wasn't noticeable. When the doors finally opened it was just him in the elevator and no evidence of the woman.

The bell rang once he reached the lobby. Daniel placed the V in his pocket and casually walked out of the elevator as soon as the doors opened. He walked up to the receptionist desk to check out of his room. She looked at him concerned but Daniel avoided eye contact with her. He remembered he was just in a tussle in the elevator, and he looked rough from that.

"You are all checked out sir," The Russian receptionist added with a warm smile.

Daniel smiled back at her and quickly left the hotel without looking back. And once he was outside, he dropped the purse and shoes of the woman who he killed in the elevator.

Chapter Three

"*W*hat the hell are you doing here?*"* Daniel sees Dock standing outside the motel as soon as he walks out the door.

Dock made a handgun gesture, *"Bang! You're dead Daniel Benson."*

Benson just stood frozen, not moving a muscle. His face went from worry to anger. *"What's this supposed to be? Cops and robbers? If you have any more information, tell me or get in line."*

Dock said, *"Peace man, relax. I'm going to make you an offer you can't refuse. Ha! I've always wanted to say that. Do you want to hear me out comrade?"*

"I'm listening and I'm not your fucking comrade," said Daniel.

"Klaus knows you're coming, so he got a big backup. He has a bodyguard named Boris Time." Dock continued *"Time was a former Russian mafia informant for me. Till that bastard turned his back on me, took the drug, and now is a minion for Klaus."*

"Good! A real fight and challenge. Speaking of which I saw how v works but I'm telling you first before I tell Invictus." He told Dock.

Then Benson went into his pocket, got out the drug and handed it to Dock. Dock took the little bottle of v and with a confused look, handed it back to Daniel.

"I hope you can find out where the blood is coming from. But yes, call the Invictus Society and tell them you must leave for Rome instantly. Till then Dasvidaniya Dhampir."

Dock then took something out of his jacket like a smoke bomb threw it on the ground and poof he was gone.

"I got to learn how to do that." Benson jokily said.

Daniel reached for his phone to give an update on the Invictus Society. April, Gina and the head boss were all on video chat.

"Any updates Daniel?" The boss announced.

"Yes, I did I found the drug lap. It is in Vatican, city in the Vatican under it. I already killed a woman she had the drug v on her. It looks like little eye drops I don't know how or when it takes effect, but I had to do what I had to do." Confessed Daniel.

"We understand, so how do you know Klaus's drug lab is under the Vatican?" asked Gina.

"I'm a former cop remember. A former private detective, I have one of those cop feeling things, and plus it's called evidence. So, half of Klaus's lab was in Russia, now I'm heading to the airport to go to Rome, Italy. If you need me, you know where to find me." Said Benson.

Daniel hangs up the phone and called Smith to pick him up from the hotel and to take him to the airport for his journey to Rome, Italy.

Midafternoon on October 7th. Daniel arrived in Rome, Italy. Daniel was waking up from his sleep when he received a phone call. He quickly grabbed his phone to answer it, first looking at the caller ID. It was Dock.

"Yes Dock?" Daniel answered.

"I notice you made it to Rome. I left you a gift at the hotel desk. It is with the clerk it's blueprints and some directions on where to go and get some rocket launchers. This is your last chance to kill all three of them and to get rid of the drugs, I'll be watching you good luck." Dock told him then the phone went dead on the other line.

Daniel looked at his watch and it was four p.m., his stomach was gurgling. He hasn't eaten anything for a few days. After he got dressed, he went to find a restaurant that had some steak or just anything bloody to crave his hunger. The blood pills worked, but only for two to three days, then he gets his cravings for blood.

After Daniel found a restaurant, he waited for the Maître D to show him where he would sit at. After the Maître D pointed at a table where Daniel could sit down, Daniel thanked him and waited for the server to come to him.

After a few minutes, a very young man approached him. *"Good evening signore. (sir) My name is Pierre and I'll be your waiter. May I start you off with something to drink?"* Pierre asked Daniel in his thick Italian accent.

"Just a glass of red wine and do you have any steak?" Benson asked his waiter.

"Ah yes, we do have the best steak in Italy. Would you like that?" asked Pierre.

"Yes, and I would like it bloody." Daniel told him.

Pierre paused for a minute thinking Benson was joking. *"Ah, you Americans are funny. Now, how would you like it signore?"* He asked him again.

"I told you bloody! You can cook it, just leave it bloody and I'm not joking. I still want the steak mooing and moving, got it?" He told his waiter.

"Si signore, I'll give you your wine right away." Pierre told Benson.

As Pierre walked away. Daniel began scoping the restaurant out to see if he could find or spot Klaus, Koi, or Rebecka. He reached inside his leather jacket pocket and took out the pictures of what they looked like. Then he used his powers to see if they were in town. He can't get inside Klaus, Koi, or Rebecka's head because they have blocked him from their minds so Daniel can't talk to them or see them.

A few minutes later Pierre came back with Daniel's glass of red wine. *"I'll go check your steak,"* replied Pierre.

He just nodded and kept scoping the restaurant out. Another few minutes went by, and Daniel didn't see them. He put the pictures back inside his leather jacket pocket and drank some of his wine. When Daniel got done drinking his wine, he saw Pierre coming towards him with his steak.

Pierre placed the steak down in front of Daniel and asked, *"How's this, signore?"*

After making sure the steak was to his liking Daniel replied to Pierre. *"Grazie"* (thank you)

Pierre nodded with satisfaction and went away.

Daniel went to town on that steak. He hadn't eaten anything that good in a long time. The baked potato with the butter and chives was heaven sent. Pierre returned occasionally to check on Daniel to make sure he was still happy with his dinner and to refill his wine glass.

Pierre returns one last time to retrieve Daniels empty plate and give him his ticket. Pierre's eyes widen when he sees that Daniel has wiped the plate clean. The waiter came back and announced. *"Signore, you must have an appetite. Especially for someone who eats a bloody steak like that. You must be a vampire."* Pierre jokingly laughs.

Benson just smiled and told him *"That's how I like my steak. Thank you again. Here is your tip."* He handed Pierre a hundred dollars.

Pierre just smiled at him gratefully, and he went towards the kitchen to return the dirty dishes. The Maître D noticed Daniel after he paid for his food. They both smiled at each other before Daniel walked out of the building.

Daniel looked at his watch, it was almost six and the sun was beginning to set. Now that he was full of energy and ready to kick ass, he was heading to the St Peter's Basilica Cathedral in Vatican City. With Benson's powers he can now fly. So instead of being there in fifty-eight minutes in a car, he would be there in twenty minutes.

Twenty minutes later Benson made it to Vatican City. It was dark by now and the Cathedral was closed. Due to the cold, there were hardly any people out. Benson ran and climbed on top of a roof building to see a better view of the Cathedral. Daniel made it to the top of the roof, and he could see Smith who was already in the city waiting for him, he took out his phone can called smith.

"Are you here?" He asked Smith.

"Yes sir, I'm here in the street with your bags of weapons sir." Smith told him.

"I'll be right down," Benson replied.

They both hung up the phone and Daniel was still on top of the roof. He walked off the ledge. He was able to fly and land safely with his new powers.

As soon as he landed on the street, Smith opened the trunk of the car so he could get his weapons. Once Daniel got all set to go to Klaus's underground drug lab, he went to Smith and reached out his hand to shake it.

"Thank you for everything. Now, get out of here kid." Daniel told Smith.

Smith nodded, then shut the trunk of the car. Smith then opened the car door, shut it then once he was in, started it up, and hauled ass.

Once Benson saw the red lights of the car gone, he loaded up his guns and his sword. He thought about his daughter Leah being in a coma and that made him angry. When he gets angry it only took seconds for his fangs to pop out and his eyes to turn red.

Once he thought out a plan, he went to the building and looked at the blueprints. There was a hidden door behind the building. Daniel walked around to the back of the building and was instantly angry again. There was a brick wall, and not a door. *"Shit!"* He hissed. *"Fucking Dock! There is no door here!"* As he continued, he got out his phone and called up Dock. After a few rings, Dock answered the phone.

"There is no door here you son of a bitch!" Benson angrily told Dock.

"Listen, there is a trash bin on the right side of the building. We left the rocket launchers and some special binoculars for you to open that door. Good luck. Dock out!"

Benson shook his head at the phone before placing it in his pocket. He then went to the right side of the building and saw the trash bin. He opened it up and true to Dock's word, there were two rocket launchers, and the binoculars Dock had mentioned.

After he grabbed everything, Benson went back to the building. He put the Binoculars against the wall and these Binoculars could see through walls. Benson could see the door. There were a few minions standing by the door as well.

"So, I'm guessing I'm going to blow up the door with these." He told himself as he turned his head to where the rocket launchers were on his back. *"Say hello to my little friends."* he added as he stood a few feet back to get ready to blow up the wall and the door. He pulled the trigger, and the rocket took off making a loud noise.

BOOOOM!

The wall was gone.

He grabbed the other rocket launcher, and he did the same.

BOOOOM!

The door was gone.

Chapter Four

The wall just exploded. The rockets blew off the wall and the door leaving a big hole along with the minions who were dead. As Benson was walking to the Cathedral, fire and smoke was on the wall and inside of the church, he dropped off the empty launchers and took out his gun, whatever minions were still alive he shot them with the special holy water bullets.

"KLAUS!" He yelled. *"KLAUS YOUR WORST NIGHTMARE IS HERE!"* Benson announced as he searched for the basement door.

He heard a voice behind him. *"No, I'm YOUR worst nightmare,"* added the unfamiliar Russian voice.

Daniel then replied, *"No. me waking up without my enormous cock is my worst nightmare."*

"You got jokes American. You must be the day walker? Turn around so you can see the man who will kill you."

Daniel did what he was told. He turned around and it was Boris Time. He was about six feet eight inches tall. All muscles, beard, long hair, wearing a black jacket with a white shirt. With black pants and boots.

"Ah you must be Boris. I'm looking for your boss." Benson told him. Time had his gun pointed at Daniel. He reached for a bag

that was next to the wooden chairs of the church, he untied the bag, and he pulled out a head.

"Here he is," confessed Time with a devious smile. He then pulled out the head of Klaus.

Whoever killed him must have wanted all the drugs for themselves. Daniel thought to himself.

"Who did this? Was it you or the other two?" He asked Boris.

"Klaus paid me good. But Koi and Rebekah paid me better once I got my payment from both of them, I took out their partner," Boris confessed.

"Where the hell are they and where are the drugs?" Benson demanded to know.

"You're too late. They left and they took the drugs with them on the ship. I believe they told me they were heading to the United States. A place called New York City." Boris admitted to it. *"And they told me, if the day walker happens to show up, they will pay me handsomely to kill him or her for them. So, I'm going to tell you what I told Klaus. Tell the devil your time has ran out."* Boris dropped the head of Klaus and took out his other gun and began shooting at Benson.

Daniel moved out of the way just in time and took out his gun. They both started shooting inside of the church. After some bullet fire and moving around, Benson finally got Boris. Got him right in the heart and Time went down like a sack of potatoes. Boris was still breathing a little bit when Benson approached him,

Daniel bent down next to Time and explained, *"You get a minute of fame for a lifetime of saving the world. You get a lifetime of infamy for a minute destroying it."*

Boris replied, *"Shut up! Shut up! Shut the fuck up!"* As he laid there bleeding out.

Daniel stood on his feet and grabbed his sword from behind his jacket. He told Boris one last thing, *"You told me to tell the devil that my time has ran out. Well, you better tell the devil that YOUR time has ran out!"* Benson then chopped off Boris's head.

Daniel then heard the sirens of the police officers coming. *"Shit I have to get to the basement quick!"* He hurried to the basement door, it was unlocked, and he then hurried down the stairs to the basement. When he got there, he realized Dock was right. There was a drug lab inside of the Church. Not only that, but Daniel found lots of paperwork on what the Vatican was hiding from the public all of these years. He wanted to go through all of it. Maybe he can capture the people who runs the Vatican and who controls the public. Benson also found other drug equipment, but the drugs were gone. Benson was pissed and started destroying the room. Papers and equipment fell violently to the floor. He called up Dock to break the news. After a few rings Dock finally answered.

"You find the drugs? Did you destroy them?" asked Dock.

"No, I missed them. Klaus is dead Boris killed him, but I killed Boris. Koi and Rebekah took a ship with the drugs, and they are heading to New York." Benson told Dock.

"Call the Invictus Society. I'll see you in New York." Dock just hung up on Benson.

"That Russian bastard doesn't let me get a word in." Benson hissed angrily.

Daniel was about to head upstairs to leave but it was too late. The police showed up and surrounded the building. He noticed a police officer was standing right next to the door. *"Well let's see if this works."* he said out loud as he started to do a chant. He was able to control the police officer's mind. He told the cop to fight with the other cops. The officer did what he was made to do. He started fighting with the other cops. Now that they were all distracted, Benson opened the door and hurried to the hole in the wall. Once he was in the clear he let go of the cop's mind and the cop went back to normal as he asked his fellow cops what happened and why he was in cuffs. As soon as Daniel got a good distance away from the cops, he called the Invictus Society.

"Any word Benson? Did you get Klaus and the drugs?" Gina asked eagerly.

"No, he is dead. His partners killed him, and they took the drugs with them. They are heading to New York right now as we speak. We must prepare for the next step. I'm going to get ahold of Smith and take the redeye back." Daniel answered her and then hung up before she could say anything else.

October 8th. New York City, New York. When Daniel got back to New York, he wanted to go to the shipping docks to find the name of the ship and whatever other evidence he could find, but the boss of the Invictus Society told him he needed to go home and get some rest. It took a lot of words back and forth, but Daniel finally agreed to go to his loft. It was the safest place for him in New York. It was deserted and unlisted. Nobody would have been able to find him there.

Daniel got up from his bed and was hurting bad. Every time he goes to battle, he has new scratches or wounds. He has some on his chest, stomach, and on his back. He washed his face and brushed his teeth. He noticed the five o' clock shadow on his face and he decided to leave it. He may be part vampire, but he can still see himself in the mirror. After taking a few blood pills to satisfy his hunger, He started to get dressed. He was startled when one of his pictures fell off the dresser. When he picked it up, he turned it over so he could see the picture. It was a picture of him, Rebecca, and Leah as a baby. The old black and white photo had seen better days. It was beginning to get more damaged. It was Benson's good luck charm. After he put the picture back on the dresser, he went to his closet. Inside the closet was his long brown trench coat, his dad's Fedora hat, and his dad's gun. He even kept John Dillinger's old tommy gun. Benson closed his eyes for a minute and started to think about that unfaithful night when he died and came back to life. He was doing good work, he smiled, and he closed the closet door to finish getting ready. He had to go to the Invictus Society's underground bunker to see if there had been any leads and to see his daughter Leah.

After a twenty-minute drive, Daniel arrived at the underground bunker of the Invictus Society. The Society had to disguise their building with a regular building so people and vampires or other supernatural beings would not find them. Once he arrived, he hit the elevator door, and he was greeted by Doctor Andrea Lovato and her Nurse Carla Mesa.

Daniel laid on the table to be examined. by the doctor and nurse.

"How are you feeling? Do you need anything? Stitched up or just time to heal?" The doctor asked Daniel as she continued to check on him.

"Just the same old cuts and bruises. I do need more blood pills. Blood type B positive." He mentioned to her.

Lovato nodded her head and motioned Carla to go to the refrigerator to get the pills. A few seconds later Carla came back with the pills and handed them to the doctor, which Andrea handed over to Benson.

After Daniel finished with his checkup and taking bloodwork for some samples, he left the doctor's office and headed to the other room to see his daughter Leah.

Once he opened the curtains to Leah's room, he sat down next to her and held her hand and began talking to Leah. He told her about his day and the mission he was on. Leah, who is a full-grown young adult, had the breathing tubes and all the machines to keep her alive while the Invictus Society were trying to do anything and everything to wake her up.

"Hi honey. It's me, your daddy. I hope you are still having good dreams about us, your mom and me. Please wake up. If you wake up, I'll let you have all the candy you want and soda. I'll let you have a boyfriend, and I won't get mad about it either." He bribed her. Deep down he knew his words weren't going to wake her up. This was the only thing that could break his heart. He let go of her hand and brushed the hair off of her face with his fingers.

After a few minutes of doing that, he got up from his chair, kissed Leah's forehead, then grabbed her hand and kissed it gently. As he was leaving, he stopped and turned around one more time to look at Leah. He mentioned to her, *"I love you baby. Please fight and wake up."* He grinned at Leah as he looked at her beauty, he noted about how she looks like her mom without the hair color. As he left her room, he wanted to cry but he couldn't shed a damn tear. The last time he cried was in 1930 when Rebecca wanted a divorce from him on their ten-year wedding anniversary. Some gift he got.

Daniel then walked down the hall to a restricted area where it was heavily guarded. As soon as Benson stopped, the two guards let him pass and the doors opened. The doors opened, and the room was full of supernatural beings. It is where they kept their prisoners. Werewolves, demons, and ghosts, but Benson just ignored them all and went straight to a special cell where Akasha was being held. She was still a stone, and she was still in the pose that she was when she turned to stone. Giving Benson the middle finger.

"Fucking mega bitch cunt! I know you can hear me! Let go of my daughter's soul! I want her back! I want her back NOW!" Benson yelled at Akasha. *"I know it's almost Halloween and I know what happened the last time so try me bitch. I don't know if Koi or Rebekah are helping you. I can sense your powers as soon as you wake up. I will damn well make sure I put you back down. So, if they are helping you, I will kill you and all of them motherfuckers. Then send you back to hell."* Daniel spits on Akasha's bullet proof Plexiglas cell.

He turned around away from Akasha. He heard a noise coming from her cell. Benson went back around to see what the noise was. Akasha's stone body moved. Her head was now facing Daniel. She was grinning at Daniel. Benson got pissed and gave her the double middle fingers. *"I see you bitch! I dare you; I double dare you bitch to come back to life! I will kick your mega bitch ass again. We don't have to wait around for a thousand-years bitch!"* Benson waited to see if she would move again but she didn't. He turned around to leave the restricted area. He decided to go downstairs to check on Pilar next.

Ever since Pilar became a slave to Akasha, she has not been the same. She acts crazy and eats bugs. Not even human food. Just bugs. Once he reached her cell door, she ran to the corner to hide from him.

"Pilar, come on girl, snap out of it." He continued. *"Your son."* He paused for a second. *"Your son passed away years ago. Don't you care that you left him? He had to go with his grandparents to be raised."* Benson reminded her.

Pilar came out of the dark corner, and she finally spoke to Daniel. *"You mean my son and my parents are all dead? When did they die?"* She asked in shock.

"Yes, your parents passed away in a car wreck in 1965 and your son passed away in 1990, you have four great grandkids. Do you even care about them?" He asked her.

Pilar's face dropped with pure sadness. She looked down at the floor not trying to expose her emotions to Benson. Benson knew this time he had got to her. She was finally coming around. He let out a sigh of relief.

Pilar slowly lifted her head back at him. It wasn't the sound of crying that he heard. It was Pilar's evil laugh instead. *"No, I'm glad they are all gone. I don't care about my great grandkids. I just care and love the queen mother who is going to kill you, Daniel. I'm glad she got your kid's soul. She was a little bitch anyway!"* Pilar continued to laugh.

Benson grew angry at that moment. His eyes glowed red and he was ready to put Pilar in her place. Something stopped him. His soft spot that he still had for his former secretary. Seeing her the way that she was wasn't her fault. It was Akasha's fault. The real Pilar always cared about her son and parents. She would never say that about Leah.

Chapter Five

After Benson left the restricted area, he saw Robert walking towards him. *"Hey Robert. I was just about to see you."* Daniel replied as he was adjusting his sunglasses to cover his red eyes still.

"Ah good. Are you ready to see your new bang bangs?" Robert asked him.

"Yes, let's see what you have for me." Stated Daniel. As he and Robert were both walking to the armory. Robert started to rub his temples and started shaking his head.

"Are you okay?" Daniel asked Robert.

"Yeah, I've been having these headaches for the last few days. It's nothing bad. I'll see the doctor after we are done here." Robert told Daniel.

They made their way through the doors of the armory and inside there was custom made weapons for Benson to kill vampires.

"Okay, what we got here is your Desert Eagle with special bullets. The bullet tips are made of wood and all of these bullets are blessed by the priest, Father Garcia. Next, we got the 45semi-automatics, twenty bullets, and one in the chamber. Last but not least, is the 12-gage pump shotgun. Of course, with the wooden pellets, but the pellets are made of oak. I done some

research and from what I learned is that vampires hate oak wood. If you really want to kill them, blast their heads off. The Desert Eagle and the semi will just stop them or piss them off if you don't aim for the heart. The 12-gage shotgun will blast their hearts out of their chests and shit their pants at the same time." Explained Robert.

"So, all these bullet tips or pellets will either kill them or piss them off?" He asked Robert.

"Yes, and if you want to do some real wet work, I just finished this baby." He replied as he reached for a briefcase. After unlocking the briefcase. He opened the case, turned it around and showed the .357 magnum. *"These bullets here. I cut the tips to make them look like a cross. With one shot, KABOOM! Vampire guts, dicks, and ass everywhere. The best part is that these bullets are engraved with your loved one's name on them. What I suggest, is save these bullets when the time is right,"* he added with a big grin on his face.

"Well, you outdone yourself as always. I just hope they won't jam like the crossbow, ugh." Daniel told him.

"They won't. I tuned and fixed them. I also checked on them myself." He told Benson. As they were packing up, Daniel noticed some blueprints on Robert's desk that looked like some sort of a new weapon.

"What is this? This weapon called Black Thunder?" Benson asked Robert.

"Ah yes, my new project. It's like a bodysuit and the weapon goes on your back. All you have to do is turn it on, hit the button, and bolts of lightning shoot out. It puts one big hole in them, I just need to get your size once it's done." Said Robert. Benson just grinned at him and gave the thumbs up to Robert.

Herrera was closing the door to his shop; he was having his headaches again. *"Ouch. I'm going to go see the doctor now."* Replied Robert as he was walking away. Daniel got a call on his cell phone, it noted Dock on the caller ID.

"Please tell me you got something on the ship and the cargo." He asked Dock.

"We do. S.S. Normandy New York port harbor. Better hurry. The police are already there." Dock said before the phone went dead. Benson hurried to his car. And went to port harbor.

As New York cops surround the boat waiting for orders. A car pulls up next to one of the cop cars, NYPD detective Ally Shepard comes out. Shepard, who has been on the force for almost nine years, is in her early thirties. She's about five eight, brown hair, hazel eyes, she has no kids, never married. She is married to her job and has an athletic figure. She walked up to one of the officers holding out her badge from around her neck, with her hair tied up, and wearing her black leather jacket.

"How long has this boat been here? How come it wrecked inside of the building?" Shepard told one of the officers. *"The dock workers tried to stop it, but it was too late. We don't know if there is anybody inside."* The officer told Ally.

Then suddenly a big loud noise came from inside of the ship. Ally and some of the officers took out their guns and started to head inside of the ship. Once they all entered the ship, Ally used her hands to signal the officers to turn one way while the other two went with her. This ship was so dark, they had to use their flashlights. Meanwhile Benson was already there hiding in the shadows in case anything pops out, with his new gun ready and loaded. Once he saw Ally and the cops moving around, he had an aura sense feeling they were not alone. Ally kept walking straight, while the two cops were snatched up quickly and quietly by some minions, then he saw movement behind Ally. Daniel, who was on top of the boat, started to make his move. Once she stopped and found a closed crate of what looked like the drugs Daniel had been looking for. She was about to open the crate, but she heard guns blasting and screaming when she turned around, she had a vampire minion behind her. The minion grabbed her throat and lifted her up. She tried to shoot the creature in the face, but it was no use. Then the vampire spoke to her.

"Mmmm fresh meat. I bet you taste good!" He got close to her cheek and started to lick at it. He was about to bite into her when Benson came down from the top of the ship with his gun locked and loaded.

"Hey ugly!" He announced to the vampire and when the vampire minion turned his head.

BOOM. His head just blew up with the special shotgun bullets. Ally fell on the ground still scared. With her gun drawn at Benson. Daniel dropped his shotgun, got close to Ally, extended his arm out and spoke.

"Come with me if you want to live." She put down her gun and extended her arm to be pulled off of the ground by Benson. Ally was about to speak but they both heard hissing and screeching noises. Benson picked up his shotgun, cocked it back, and was ready to fire on the rest of the Minions. *"Get behind me now!"* He yelled to Ally. She did what she was told, but she had her gun out too just in case. Then three more vampire minions popped out of nowhere.

BOOM.
One down.
BOOM.
Two down.
CLICK.

"Fuck I'm out." He told himself as the last vampire began getting closer. He took out his Desert Eagle and started firing. He kept firing till the last wooden bullet finally got the vampire minion killing it. After Daniel got done killing all the vampires, he turned back around to Ally who still had her gun out.

"Wh... what the hell was that?" She asked.

"You wouldn't believe me if I told you. All you need to know is that I'm Daniel Benson and you are?" He asked Ally.

"Detective Ally Shepard." She answered him.

Daniel, who now has a worry look on his face replied, *"Shepard. Last time I trusted a Shepard was in 1935. He was captain for the New Orleans police."*

Ally, being confused, puts down her gun and says, *"1935? But how? Why?"*

Daniel was going to answer, but the cops that were killed started rising from the dead as vampire minions. They started going after him and Ally. Daniel got his sword from the back of his leather jacket and chopped off all of their heads with one swing; after he got done with that, he took the blood of the sword and wiped it on one of the cops bodies. Again, he turns around to talk to Ally, but she shot him in the face.

BLAM.

Benson just stood there with the bullet in his mouth. He then spits it out onto his hand to check it out.

"Hmm, I have been stabbed, but being shot in the face with this 9mm bullet is potatoes. It kind of tickles a little bit, but please don't do that again. I'm on your side." Daniel assured her.

Ally looked shocked and put her gun down again. *"What the hell are you?"* She asked him.

"Long story short. I'm a vampire hunter. I'm a Dhampir. Half human, Half vampire. Now please help me with these crates." He told her. She holstered her gun and helped him with the crate of drugs.

Once they got the drugs out of the ship, Benson and Shepard went back inside the ship to see if they could find anymore. After a few minutes of searching, they came up with nothing, just one crate.

"Fucking Koi and Rebekah." He muttered to himself. Once they both left the ship, Ally had to radio dispatch, while Benson opened the crate.

"Ah, there you are. So, you're v or vampir." Benson noted to himself. He took one of the drugs out and it has been confirmed it looks like eye drops. Once Ally got done talking to dispatch, she went to see what Benson was doing.

"What are you doing this is evidence." She told him.

"You mean WAS evidence. My bosses want this to see how it works." He explained.

Just then she took out her gun and pointed it at Daniel. *"Step away from the crate now and put your hands on top of your head."* She ordered him.

Benson stopped what he was doing, turned around and did what he was told, but Ally didn't notice he put a bomb in the crate. for it to be destroyed. *"Alright detective, I'll do what is right, but what are you going to do? arrest the guy who saved your ass or save the evidence?"* He mentioned to her. She looked confused, but then Daniel took off running. Meanwhile she went to the crate and saw the bomb in there. There were ten seconds remaining on the clock. She didn't have time left. So, she ran as fast as she could to her car and hid. Once the bomb went off, all the drugs and crate were destroyed.

Just then, the rest of the cops and her captain showed up. She tried to look for Daniel, but he was nowhere to be found. Her Captain William Benjamin gets out of his car, pissed off as he slams the door he replied.

"Goddammit Ally! What the fuck happened? Get to the station and into my office now!" Her captain ordered her.

She did what she was told to do. She went to her car and drove to the station. Benson was right behind her too. He followed her to the station. Sometime later at the office of Captain Benjamin, Shepard was sitting down in the captain's office when he barges in all pissed off. He slams the door and makes his way to his desk and chair. He sat down and spoke.

"What the fuck happened out there? Dead bodies, cops with no heads, evidence blown up! Explain yourself Shepard."

"I don't know. Dispatch called about a shipwreck. So, I went over to see what was going on. Backup took too goddamn long so; we just went inside of the ship and shit went down. I had one suspect, but he got away. He's the one who blew up the crate and he took some evidence." She explained to him.

"What does he look like?" He asked her.

"I don't know, like a broke ass homeless John Wick. Wearing all black and I mean all black. He had a sword and sunglasses. He looked sick because of his pale ashy skin." She told her captain.

Just before he could question her, he got a phone call on his office phone. "What!" Then he calmed down.

"Yes sir. Whatever you say sir. Yes sir. I'll send him in right now. No no no, I will make sure they will get along. Yes sir."

After Benjamin got off the phone he went back to talk to Ally.

"Okay Shepard it's your lucky night. I was going to suspend you without pay and take your gun, but the call I got is from a group called The Invictus Society. They are going to send in their special agent right now. And you two WILL work together whether you like it or not. Now go to your desk, he will be on his way." William told her.

She got up and was leaving the captain's office, and once she opened the captain's office door, she noticed a person sitting at her desk. They were reading the paper with their feet kicked up on her desk.

As she approached her desk, she told the person, *"Excuse me! You're in my seat."*

As soon as that person got done with the paper, they closed it revealing their face. It was Daniel. they both said, *"YOU AGAIN!"*

Chapter Six

"*C*APTAIN!" Ally yelled nervously as she got out her gun and pointed it at Daniel. She never took her eyes off of him. Daniel just got up from her seat and just stood there waiting for the captain.

A few seconds later, Benjamin came out of his office along with a few officers as well. He saw what Ally was doing. *"ALLY STAND DOWN!"* he commanded her.

"But..." she tried to speak but the captain cut her off.

"But nothing! Stand down now. This is the special agent from the Invictus Society, Daniel Benson." William informed Ally.

She paused for a minute, but then holstered her gun.

"Shepard, this will be your new partner. He is here to help with the wrecked ship at the port harbor. He is known as a Dhampir. Half human and half vampire. He is a good guy, and he will explain everything to you. Now, get out of here!" William added After that he went back to his office.

They both stood there and looked at one another. *"Homeless John Wick huh? Well, I know I need a shave and a haircut but that was fucked up. I'm like a homeless Jesus."* He joked sarcastically.

"How did you hear that if the door was closed?" she asked curiously.

"I have very good hearing, among other things, but I also have a don't fuck with me and I won't fuck with you attitude." He replied rudely as he lowered his sunglasses to reveal his red glowing eyes.

"What the fuck are you?" Ally asked frightened,

"That is a long story. I hope you are hungry because, I want pie in New Jersey?" He told her.

Ally nodded her head yes.

They both left the police station, got in Daniel's car, and started to make the hour and half drive to Jersey.

"So, are you going to tell me what you are or are we going to be quiet for the rest of the ride up to Jersey?" Ally finally broke the silence.

"Here it goes, don't fall asleep on me." He teased. *"I was a former New York cop but back in 1935. I got set up by my former partner Clark Young. It caused my divorce. I have a little girl, so I became a private detective. Which also made me become an alcoholic. I had the biggest case of my life when I found out a father from the church summoned a vampire. A mega bitch named Akasha. She went by the name Lady Deedra Benevento. She hired me to find her husband, but it was all set up just to get to my daughter. Akasha wanted a new body and to kill off the last of my bloodline. Leah, my daughter, was the perfect fit. When the mega bitch killed me, I became reborn, a Dhampir. I have a lot of powers and things that I can do that vampires can't. For instance, going to churches and walking in the sun. My nickname is Day Walker."* Benson told her his story.

"So, do you kill and feed on people too?" asked Ally as she covered her neck.

"No, I can eat human food. I take blood pills for my cravings and I'm on a mission to stop the last four, well now three, vampire gods, Koi, and Rebekah, they were also another vampire named Klaus, but they killed him. They are the ones who made this drug called vampir and on top of that, all the historic people made a deal with them. My first case for the Society was Bonnie and Clyde. The case was given to me by my sister. She was part of the Invictus Society. So, you can uncover your neck. I won't bite you. I just want my pie." He replied to Ally.

After an hour and a half drive, they made it to Debbie's Diner. Debbie bought the diner from the second owners, Vincent Jr., and Jessica Morrison, back in 1970. Since then, she has remodeled it over the years. Once they reached the diner, they both went inside. It was Debbie, who was in her late sixties, with short hair, and hazel eyes, who greeted them. Danni, who also the co-owner of the diner, was also the server. She was in her mid-forties with brown hair, and blue eyes. She was born and raised in New Jersey all her life. She has worked at the diner since 2000 and is the cook as well when it's a not so busy night.

"Hello Daniel, good to see you again. Here for some pie?" asked Debbie with a big grin on her face.

"You know me all too well Debbie," Benson smiled back at her.

"New girlfriend?" She asked Benson.

"No, just a new partner. NYPD and the Invictus Society teamed up on this case. Meet Detective Ally Shepard." He introduced Ally to Debbie.

"Hello dear. Welcome to Debbie's Diner. I hope you are hungry." She told Ally.

Ally nodded her head yes and started to follow behind Benson to his usual booth. Danni was following behind them as well. Once they sat down, Danni held out her pen and pad ready to take Benson and Ally's order.

"Your usual order Hon?" Danni asked Benson.

Daniel nodded yes,

Danni began writing his order down on the pad. Then she went to Ally, *"What will you have Hon?"* Danni's New Jersey accent was thick.

"Humm, I'll just have the turkey club, with fries, along with a coffee and water please," replied Ally.

"Okay Hon. I'll put those orders in," Danni gave them both a warm smile before walking away.

"So, any other questions you want to ask me, or should we start on the case?" Benson asked Ally.

"Yeah, just one. Why the hell did you come all the way to New Jersey for pie when we could have stayed in the city?" Ally was curious to know.

Daniel paused for a minute and had a flashback. New Jersey 1919, It's the same diner run by Vincent Sr. and his wife Amanda. They also had a little boy named Vincent Jr. Daniel Benson, who was in the police academy at the time, had just got done training for the day when he walked into the diner for the first time. He searched for a seat or a booth that was available. Once he found a lonely booth at the end of the diner, he walked up to it and sat down. He grabbed the menu and glanced through it finding something that would satisfy his hunger. He wanted something tasty before he headed back to New York. He was studying the menu when a voice caught his attention.

"Hello, what will you have to drink?" asked the server in her thick Irish accent.

He looked up and saw the most beautiful young woman ever. Her hair was the color of wildfire, and she had the greenest of green eyes he had ever seen. Her name tag read Rebecca.

Once Daniel snapped out of his flashback, he mumbled to Ally, *"Just old memories, that's all."*

"Okay whatever, so does Debbie and the rest of these people know what you are as well?" Ally asked Daniel.

"Debbie, how long have I been coming here? Do you know what I am and what I do?" Daniel asked Debbie.

"Since 1919 and yes. You are a Dhampir. You like your steak very rare and bleeding still." She noted from across the diner.

"Thank you," added Benson.

A minute later Danni comes back with Ally and Daniel's orders. Once they got their food, Daniel scarfed down his rare and bloody steak.

She asked him, *"So, this is what you call your pie? A rare steak."*

"Yes, it's a code word for me. Like I mentioned, I can eat human food, but I can't get drunk off liquor or get sick. I'm immune to every sickness that there is." He explained to Ally.

Once they both finished their food and drinks, Benson tips Debbie and Danni both one hundred dollars like he has for years. As they were about to leave Daniel got a sense of something bad heading into the diner.

"You might want to take your gun out." He told Ally.

He then looked at Debbie and Danni and they already knew the look Benson was giving them. As soon as the diner door opened two guys in ski masks came barging in with shotguns. One of them shot at the ceiling while the other one spoke.

"Alright! This is a robbery. No one moves, no one gets hurt. Let's go grandma, open the register!" The robber demanded Debbie while the Second robber told Danni to get on the floor. He then pointed his gun at Shepard and Benson. Shepard was behind Daniel; she was ready with her gun. *"You two, on the floor and give me your wallet and purse. Everything you have."* The Second robber demanded Daniel and Ally.

Benson didn't do it. In fact, he just walked towards the robber.

"Hey stop! I'm gonna blast you into Kingdome come!" Confessed the masked man who now sounded not so tough.

"Do it! Come on do it I dare you, I double dare you shoot me motherfucker shoot...."

BANG

The second robber shot Daniel. Everyone saw what happened. The first robber, who was pointing the gun at Debbie, now pointed the gun at Daniel. As Benson stood where he was at, he looked down at his chest where he got shot and with his powers and energy the wounds healed up fast and quickly. Daniel just grinned at the robber who shot him and snickered, *"My turn!"* and he opened his mouth showing his fangs and he began to bite down on the robber's neck who shot him.

As both of them were on the ground the first robber was about to shoot Ally, but she was quick and shot him first. Once in the hand and the other in the shoulder. He went down like a sack of marbles. She got close to the robber she kicked the shotgun away from him and she started to handcuff him. *"Call the police."* She told Debbie.

Once she got done doing that she turned around, and she saw Benson finishing off the other robber. *"What the fuck was that? I thought you don't feed on humans?"* Shepard questioned Benson.

"I don't, but if someone is going to mess with my people, I protect them and besides, I wanted dessert. His blood type is gross, not a fan of type O." He confessed.

As Benson wiped the blood off his mouth, he walked over to the shotgun, picked it up, and handed it to Debbie. *"Take this in case, I won't be here next time."* He suggested it to her.

Then Ally picked up the robber, and then she sat him down on the table. Then he and Daniel locked eyes and Daniel began to do his magic on him. *"First you will tell the cops you snapped and bit your partner's neck. Then you will tell him you gave yourself up because I'm crazy, stupid ass and I deserve to go to jail like the punk bitch I am got it?"* He told the perp.

"Yes, I got it. I should be in jail for the rest of my life." The robber confessed. Then

Benson smiled at Debbie and Danni and left with Ally following close behind. They walked back to Daniel's car and the wind blew a cold crisp breeze. It almost made Ally shiver.

"What's the next move Daniel?" Ally asked, trying to keep her mind off being cold.

"Home. There is nothing we can do but wait and see if any dead bodies pop up, I have some evidence. Invictus Society will work on that. I'll take you back to the police station to drop you off at your car so you can go home." Benson replied.

They both got inside Daniel's car and made the hour and half drive back to New York. After the long drive back, both Benson and Shepard were tired. Once they arrived at the police station, Benson pulled up to the doors to let Ally out.

Before Ally could get out of the car Daniel explained to her, *"Listen, I'm sorry for taking the evidence, but I want to protect the people and end this nightmare for good. And hopefully see my daughter up and awake. Watch your ass and if I was you, I would get holy water or some crosses to protect you. If you get a tip, here is my cell number. I may be tired but I'm always up."* Benson handed her a piece of paper that revealed his phone number.

Ally nodded her head and grabbed the paper out of Benson's hand. She then climbed out of the car and made her way into the station. Once Benson saw Ally disappear inside the building, he got a call on his cell. He checked to see who it was before answering it.

"Hello Miss Martha. How are you?" asked Daniel.

It was Martha Redhook. Martha who has aged since they last met up in 1935. After that night, Martha Redhook moved out of New Orleans. When her mother died, she then moved to a Suburban city New York. Got married, had four kids. Two boys and Two girls. She has Two grandkids and four great grandkids. She calls Benson once in a great while to see how he is doing, but this call was more important.

"Daniel, I'm glad you answered your phone. I have a family emergency. It involves my fourth great granddaughter Amaya." Martha replied with panic in her voice. She had been using an oxygen mask to breathe for several years now. She became a smoker since 1935 and now her lungs don't work like they used to.

"What happened? What is going on with Amaya?" Daniel asked Martha.

"She left the city. She was heading to hell's kitchen in New York to do a job and we haven't heard from her since then. It's been a few weeks." She told Benson. "I'm really worried about her Daniel."

"Have the cops been involved?" He asked her.

"Yes, but the cops don't care. You know how they are." She replied as she began coughing.

"Martha, calm down okay. Send me a picture of what she looks like, okay? I'll go to Hell's Kitchen first thing tomorrow night. I promise you." He told her after a few coughs she finally calmed down.

"Okay! I'm calmed now. Please. Just help me find her."

After a few more minutes on the phone, Martha and Daniel hung up with each other. Daniel was really exhausted now. He had to go to one more place before he could head home. He had to go to the New York cemetery to talk to Rebecca.

After the thirty-minute drive, Benson climbed out of his car with some flowers from an all-night flower shop. They were yellow and pink lilies. It was Rebecca's favorite flowers. Daniel walked right to the tombstone of Rebecca Benson, he put the lilies on top of her tombstone, and he just started talking to Rebecca like she was there.

"Hey honey, I'm having a hard time trying to get our daughter to wake up, but I'm trying. I hope you are okay up there with the family. I miss you and I know you want me to be strong so, I'm trying for real I am. You should see Leah. She's all grown up now. You two would definitely be having girl time while the

son in law and I would listen to the Yankees on the radio. Or watch the game on the T. V. I wish I could cry, but I can't. I don't have any emotions. I just get more pissed off. I love you, Becky. I'm keeping my promise I made when you passed away, I'm watching our daughter till she wakes up." Benson told her.

Daniel kissed the tombstone with his hand. He then looked at his and Leah's tombstone. They all passed away in 1970 The Invictus Society did a good job with everything. They planned the funeral and how they all died. Out of nowhere ice-cold rain fell from the sky, interrupting Daniels train of thought.

"Fucking vampires!" Benson announced out loud.

He recently found out that the vampires can control the weather amongst other things. He went back to his car and went home to his loft to try to get some shut eyes and start out fresh tomorrow.

October 9th, six p.m. As Benson was getting up from his slumber, he had a few missed calls. Some from Martha, Dock, and the Invictus Society. He called Dock first.

"What do you have for me Dock?" asked Benson.

"Ah Daniel we may have a lead on where Koi and Rebekah are at. They have a nightclub in hell's kitchen in New York. It's called 'The Nipple Clamps.' We believe the drugs might be in there. We are afraid they are going to start handing them out to every drug dealer they come in contact with. We will send you more info on them right now. Good luck." Dock told him. The phone went silent after that.

Benson then called Martha.

"Daniel, have you found my fourth great granddaughter yet? Did you get her info I sent you on your phone?" asked Martha.

"I just got it now Martha. Where was she working at in hell's kitch..." Daniel paused as he was looking at the information Martha sent him. Amaya works at The Nipple Clamps. "Son of a bitch Martha. Amaya is working with vampires! I'm going to get her tonight I promise you." Benson promised Martha.

"Thank you. Please get her back to me safe and sound." Martha pleaded with Daniel.

"I will." He told her. After he got done talking on the phone with Martha, he called the Invictus Society and Gina answered the call.

"Hello Daniel, we have news about Koi and Rebekah. We have your new partner here as well. We also know how this drug works. See you soon." Then Gina hung up the phone.

After Daniel made all of his calls, he got dressed, loaded up his guns, put his sword behind his back, and left his loft. He got in his car and headed to the Invictus Society building.

Chapter Seven

After a thirty-minute drive from Benson's loft. He arrived at the Invictus Society building. He took the elevator down to their underground. The doors opened, and Ally was standing there waiting for him along with the doctor and Robert.

"*Alright everyone. I'm here. What do you have on this drug doc?*" He asked Doctor Lovato.

"*We did some testing on this drug and it's weird. We did it on the mice and nothing. But once we found some homeless people to volunteer, shit went weird.*" She said.

"*Subject one, we put one drop in both eyes, and he turned into a vampire within one hour. Subject two, we put two eye drops in both eyes and he turned a bit quicker. Five minutes. Subject three, we put three eye drops in both of his eyes and he turned within thirty seconds. So, whoever's blood this is, it turns normal people into these ugly fucks,*" explained Doctor Andrea.

"*I've seen this before. They are minions. They are the army of the head vampires.*" Benson told Lovato.

"*What do you want to do? They are still alive and going crazy in their bullet proof glass cells.*" Lovato replied to Benson.

"*I have killed them a few times. Let me handle them. Do you still have the eye drops?*" He asked her.

"*No, they are with the homeless people.*" She answered.

Benson took his hand out and ordered the doctor to give him the keys. "*Give me a moment. Watch the camera,*" he told them.

"*I'll go with you,*" insisted Ally.

"*No, you watch the camera. You don't know what you are doing*!" He angrily told Shepard.

Ally did what she was told. They all watched the camera to watch Benson do his work. After a few minutes later, Benson went to each subjects cell and chopped off each of their heads. When he was done, he went to the medical room where everyone was waiting.

"*Are you hurt? Do I need to check you for anything? You know it's the rules. I have to take blood samples from you.*" Lovato told Benson.

"*No but do what you got to do. I don't know why you have to do this shit every fucking time*!" Daniel protested against the doctor.

April and Gina walked in the room while Ally was getting checked out by Carla.

"*Here you go. Here are the files on Koi and Rebekah, and the location of their club, The Nipple Clamps,*" Gina handed the file to Daniel.

Daniel grabbed the file from Gina as he was getting checked out by Andrea. He checked out the files and blueprints on where to go and where to enter. Daniel nodded his head to accept the mission.

The Doctor took some blood and more samples from Daniel and Ally. They both then collected some guns and bullets from Robert. They were now good to go.

Benson looked at Robert. "*Are you okay? It looks like you haven't slept in the last few days. Are you having nightmares or what is going on?*" He questioned Robert.

"*NOTHING!*" He yelled at Benson.

"*What the fuck is wrong with you. Either you need iron in your diet, or you need to get pussy. Pick one but don't yell at me like that again or I'll kick your fucking ass myself.*" Benson warned Robert.

"*I'm sorry. I just have not been myself. I'm going to go home now, but once I feel better, I need your partner. I need her measurements for the Black Thunder project.*" Herrera replied.

After that argument. Shepard and Benson made their way to the elevator. Once they got on, Benson was about to press the button to go up until he saw Carla running towards them.

"*Hey, you forgot your pills. Lovato made this for you as well.*" She told him before handing him something. It was a gun that had blood in it. In case Benson ran out of pills he could pop it in his neck and pull the trigger.

"*Thank you, Carla, but can you do me a favor? Watch out for Robert. I don't like the way he has been acting.*" He asked her.

She nodded yes before the elevator doors closed.

Benson then pushed the button to go up to leave the building.

Once they left the building, they got in Daniel's car and took the twenty-minute drive to Hell's Kitchen where The Nipple Clamps nightclub was located.

It was nine o clock when Daniel and Shepard found the club. There was a line from the door to the end of the block.

"*How do you want to do this?*" Shepard asked him.

"Well, first hide your badge, and let's look at the blueprints." He suggested to her.

Ally hid her badge under her shirt. They both went over the plan. *"I see some heating system under the building and an electric fuse box. I have some c4 in the trunk of my car and the detonator to go with it. You go around to the back building, sneak downstairs, and plant the c4, then wait on my signal."* He explained to her. He then reached into the glovebox to give her an earpiece to put in her ear.

"Wait a minute! Why do you have c4 in the back of your car?" She questioned Benson.

"Oh, you know, in case the neighborhood kids want to play with c4." Benson joked being a wiseass to her. *"In case of shit like this. Now can we focus."*

Ally shook her head, then put her earpiece in her ear. She then cocked back her gun to be loaded. *"And what about you? How are you going to get in?"* She asked Daniel.

"Me? I'm going to play Bogart like I've done hundreds of times." He told Ally.

"Who?" She asked him confused.

"Never mind let's go." He told Ally.

They both opened the car doors and shut them, then they both went their separate ways after Ally grabbed the c4 out of the trunk.

"Can you hear me? If you can. Watch your ass." Benson told her.

"Yes, watch yours as well," she replied.

Daniel walked right up to the club where a really big bouncer was standing outside. Daniel reached into his pocket to grabbed a rolled-up wad of cash. It was at least one thousand dollars. Benson cut everyone in line when he saw the bouncer who was white and bald and at least over six feet tall all muscle.

"*Hey little man, you can't come in here unless you're on the list.*" The bouncer said to Daniel.

"*I'm on the list. My friends and I are on the list.*" He told the bouncer while he showed him the money and then he hypnotized him.

"*You are on the list. Go on in and have a good time.*" Replied the bouncer who took the money from Benson.

He went inside the club, he stopped using his powers and the bouncer and he went back to normal. After Daniel was inside of the club it was a packed house. He got out his phone and started looking for Martha's fourth great granddaughter Amaya. He asked the workers and wait staff, and they hadn't seen her or didn't know her by that name. Then Daniel went up to the bartender and announced, "*excuse me, have you seen this woman?*" He asked.

He was showing the picture of Amaya.

"*You mean Santanico Serpent?*" asked the bartender.

"*Yes her,*" he replied.

"*She's about to perform in a few minutes, if you can find a seat so you can see her.*" The bartender pointed towards the stage.

Daniel walked away and looked for a table. Once he found one. He kicked off the passed-out dude onto the floor and he sits down right in the front row.

A few minutes later, here comes the bartender walking on stage with a microphone. "*Okay you filthy dogs. The moment you have been waiting for. Get on your knees, you dog and beg for her as The Nipple Clamps welcomes Santanico Serpent,*" announced the bartender.

The stage went dark, and a spotlight came on. The curtains opened and sure as shit, it was Amaya, every guy and woman just opened their mouths and was quiet. Daniel was amazed by how she looked. She had black hair, long muscle legs, a flat six pack stomach, size D breast, and her eyes! Her hazel sparkling eyes that could hypnotize a motherfucker. She took off her robe and was wearing black bra and black thong panties. She had a Native American headband all the way down to her body. She took that off as well. Then, the band started to play. While the band was playing, she was dancing sexy and grinding on a stripper's pole. Then two bouncers helped her down on the stage. Then Amaya walked slowly towards Benson with her eyes locked on him. Out of everyone in this club, she chose him. Her hands slowly caressed her breast all the way to her thighs. She reached Benson and slowly sat on his lap with her back against his chest. Her hips moved to the beat of the music. Everyone in the club disappeared and it was just them two. Benson's heart almost pounded out of his chest. He was nervous. She knew Daniel wanted her, yet she still chose to play with him. She grabbed both his hands and placed them around her stomach. Her abs were tight. She wrapped her arms around his neck, and her head rested on his shoulder. As she was bending over, Benson noticed she had a tattoo on her lower back, all the way around to her ass cheeks. It was a long black dragon. She then turned her body around facing him. Her arm was on his shoulder while the other one was making its way to his cock to make it hard. Her body moved slowly, and it made him want her right then and there.

She went close to Daniels ear and whispered to him, "Meet *me in the back."* She then finished her dance. Once the band was done playing, she climbed off Daniel and disappeared off stage.

The crowd went wild. Clapping and whistling. Daniel was frozen from amazement. He couldn't do anything but gush. "Now *that was a fucking show."* He said out loud and started clapping with the rest of the guys.

He then heard Ally. "*Hey, Benson, I have been reaching and calling you. What the fuck happened to you? Are you okay?"* She asked. Benson went to his ear and spoke.

"*Yes, I got distracted. Is everything set up?"* He asked.

"*Yes, what now?"* She asked.

"*Get the hell out of there and wait for my signal."* He told Shepard.

"*What are you going to do?"* She asked Daniel,

"*I need to find Koi and Rebekah to see if they are here. And get these people out of here too,"* replied Benson.

"*Do you need backup? Should I call for backup?"* She asked Benson.

"*No, let's not freak out these people here. I need to find one more person. Just wait and be ready. Benson out."* He replied.

Ally had no choice but to agree to his plan. She waited for Benson to signal.

Meanwhile, he had to get in the back somehow to find Amaya. He found one of the bodyguards guarding the back. Benson made his move. He got close to the bodyguard. "*Hey, pal, some asshole is starting shit in the bathroom. I think he is high on drugs."* He told him.

"*Ugh! I swear I hate this fucking job. Thank you, sir, I will handle it."* The bodyguard told him.

Once the bodyguard left, the backroom was unguarded. He opened the curtains to the back, and he went inside. Once Benson was inside of the back of the club, he noticed lots of music equipment, people walking, and staying in the back talking to other people. He found a few dressing rooms empty or not the right one. But once he found Amaya's it was go time. He unholstered his weapon. He tried the doorknob, but it was locked. Before he could kick the door down, he saw some light coming from the keyhole. Once he saw Amaya, he had to find a way in there. Once Daniel got back up on his feet, he thought he could knock. Before he could do that, someone tapped him on the shoulder. Once Daniel turned around it was the bodyguard, but he turned into the vampire minion.

"*Ah shit.*" Benson said as the bodyguard grabbed him by the throat. He was taking him towards the back of the building where a secret elevator was. Benson tried his best to escape but the bodyguard's grip, but he was just too strong for him. Once the elevator dinged and the doors opened, the bodyguard just tossed Benson in there. Benson, who still had his weapon on him tried to shoot the bodyguard, but the bodyguard's strength didn't affect the bullets hitting him. Once Benson got up on his feet the bodyguard just pushed a button and left, leaving Benson alone in the elevator.

Once the elevator dings the doors open, he saw another minion bodyguard. Once he saw that. He aimed his gun, but the bodyguard grabbed Daniel's gun quickly and broke it. After he did that, he grabbed Daniel by the throat again. He was being carried by his throat taking him to a big, long office with cameras all around the club. There was a big desk, and one person was watching the cameras on a chair and the other was standing up next to the person sitting on the chair. Once the bodyguard let go of Benson, he fell to the ground. Benson started gasping for air.

"*Ah, welcome Daniel Benson or should we call you Day Walker?*" asked a deep voice Benson didn't recognize.

They both turned around revealing their glowing reddish yellowish eyes. It was none other than Koi and Rebekah. Koi, who was sitting down, was a pale male with bleach blond hair. He was wearing a nice red and black suit with a red tie. While Rebekah, who was black, with dreadlocks, was wearing a long black dress and holding a doll that looked like Benson.

Once Benson caught his breath and was back on his feet, he went for his back up gun.

"*I wouldn't do that if I was you,*" warned Koi.

He stopped what he was doing.

Rebekah started admiring him. "*My, you are a good looking Dhampir. Very handsome man. Where have you been all my life?*" Rebekah giggled.

"*Working on my tan.*" Benson replied sarcastically.

"*Now do not be cute. Guard! Bring him to me!*" Rebekah yelled to the guard.

The guard grabbed Daniel behind the neck, picking him off the ground and walked towards Rebekah. Once the guard did that, he let's go of Daniel and the guard stood close by. Rebekah walked close to Benson, and she grabbed his cock and spoke.

"*What have you been feeding this thing?*" She asked him.

"*Redheads.*" He joked with her.

"*Well, I think he needs a change.*" She replied as she smiled at him.

Benson was just frozen solid and didn't move a muscle. Rebekah grabbed Benson's hand and started to kiss it. Then she grabbed a dagger and cut open his hand to get some of his blood. Daniel yelped for a bit until Rebekah started to drink his blood from the wound she made.

"*Mmmmm it's pure and fresh.*" She told Koi. She began putting some of Benson's blood on the doll.

A minute later Amaya walked inside the office.

"*Ah! Santanico perfect timing. What can you tell us about this day walker? Tell us powerful witch!*" Replied Koi.

Daniel turned around and it was Amaya. She was all in black and she was pierced, she had 3 rings in her right eyebrow and a chain from her ear connected to her nose. She had a black mini top on with black leather pants and black boots.

Amaya looked into Daniel's eyes. She put her hands on top of his temples, and she started seeing visions from his past.

Chapter Eight

After she got done reading Daniel's vision she turned around and announced to Koi and Rebekah. *"This is him. The one the prophet one. He is the one who killed all the Gods of Vampires. And he knows where the Queen Akasha is. We can finally free her and the four of you can all rule the world."*

Benson, who had a confused look on his face, *"Four? I only see two vampires and after I kill both of them, I'm going to kick your ass. Santanico or whoever you are bitch."* He threatened Amaya.

Amaya did a low kick on his legs and Benson fell off his feet and onto the ground. After she did that, she got on top of Daniel. She held his hands on top of his head, so he couldn't move. Amaya went close to his ear and whispered.

"I know my fourth great grandma is looking for me. She told me stories about you. I am undercover as well. So be a good little boy and let me handle this." She told him and after that she went close to Daniel's face, got close to his lips and she kissed him hard.

"Problem Santanico?" asked Koi.

"No. No problem at all. Just looking for more weapons, but I think I found a weapon I like more." She told Koi. She then leaned into Benson and whispered in his ear, *"Now once I let*

go of your arms, I want you to hit me hard. I know you have the building rigged to blow up. I'm ready and I hope you are ready too."

He nodded his head yes.

As soon as Amaya let go of Daniel's arm, he coldcocked her with a big punch to knock her out.

Koi and Rebekah saw what happened and they called the guards to get Benson. As he saw the guards running towards him, he did a kip up. Pulled out his knifes from behind his back and slashed both guards' throat's. He took out his back up gun and pointed it at Koi and Rebekah.

"Where's the drug's coming from? Whose blood, is it? You or cock grabber?" He asked them.

They both began to laugh. Daniel was still holding his gun at both of them. Then he picked up Amaya grabbed her by her neck and pointed his gun at her that's when they both stopped laughing.

"You are a fucking fool, it is not from Rebekah, or I. It is a special blood from Dr. Justin Drake. He is waiting for Queen Akasha to wake up so we can all rule the world." Koi confessed.

"What does he look like and where is he?" asked Benson.

"We will never tell you. When the clock strikes midnight on Halloween, these humans are fucked, and we shall rule the world." Replied Koi.

Koi and Rebekah began walking towards Daniel slowly.

Daniel was close to a window. He could break it and him, and Amaya could jump out the window and make it out safe. "ALLY NOW!" Yelled Benson into his earpiece.

Then all of a sudden, the building started to rattle, and flames were coming out of the walls. Koi and Rebekah didn't know what to do. They just looked at Benson.

With a smile on his face, he told both of them. "*Hasta La Vista baby.*" He put Amaya over his shoulder and jumped out of the window while Koi and Rebekah still stood where they were at. Daniel and Amaya were falling out the window and Benson landed on his feet like a cat. He shook Amaya up to let her know the coast was clear.

"*Wake up. It is okay now.*" He told Amaya.

"*Kiss me.*" She whispered.

Daniel dropped her just to get her going. "*You got to earn my respect to kiss these thunder lips.*" He told Amaya.

Amaya was getting up from the ground wiping the dirt off her. "*Geez, are you always the asshole when you rescue a damsel in distress?*" She asked him.

"*Not when the damsel is working for the enemy. Want to tell me what the hell is going on? And who the fuck you work for?*" He asked Amaya.

As they began to walk to Daniel's car she began to talk.

"*I work for a secret society that handles a lot of cases from all around the world. My grandmother taught me to use powers and whatnot because of my Native America culture. When I was twenty-one, fourth great Grandmother Martha told me about you and the group. She used to work for the Invictus Society. Once I heard about them, I wanted to work for them, but they told me no. I'm with another group, but unlike your group, we do the work and trust the vampires. Unlike you, you kill. Mister you shoot first and ask questions later.*" She confessed to him.

"What group do you work for? Maybe we can work together and figure out who's blood is in the drug and end this nightmare." Benson suggested to her.

"I'll think about it." She told him. As she got close to him. She was about to kiss Daniel again, but here came Ally yelling at Benson.

"Daniel did we get them?" Shepard asked.

Daniel turned his head to see Ally for a quick second and then he turned around to see Amaya was gone. *"Motherfucker! I really need to learn how to do that."* He snickered to himself.

Ally got closer to Daniel she asked, *"Who was that?"*

Daniel said, *"I think I'm in love."*

"Are you okay?" Ally asked him.

"I'm fine. Let's just hope Koi and Rebekah are dead. Hopefully they burned up in the fire so we can find the source of the drug. I have a name, but don't know what he looks like or who he is." Benson replied to Shepard.

"We need to report to the Invictus Society."

October 11th after taking a day off for recovery. Daniel and Ally were ready to get back at it. They agreed to meet at the building of the Invictus Society. Ally was already inside the building in the medical room with the doctor and her nurse. As she was getting blood work and some DNA as per requested by the Invictus Society. When Ally was all done, the curtains opened up and it was Benson. Something was different about him.

"What? What are you all looking at?" He asked the three of them who were just staring at him. He had cut his hair and now had clean-shaven face.

"Who is she?" asked Andrea.

"No one! Can a guy get a shave and a haircut? Tired of looking like a hobo bum all the time." He replied.

"Bullshit! It was that stripper from the club from the other night," said Shepard.

"ALRIGHT FINE! It was her. She did something to me that, I have never felt. Since I first met my wife. And for your information Ally, she's a dancer not a stripper." He told her.

"Now can we get to work after this shit. I'm getting really tired of this ugh." He told everyone.

Everyone began laughing and joking about Daniel. Ally got a call on her cell phone. She

looked at her phone and it was her job, so, she answered it. While walking away to take the call. Benson got up on the table to take bloodwork.

"Let me ask you something doc? Why do you have to take my blood and my samples?" He asked Andrea.

"I don't know. I wish I could tell you. But they give me the orders; I do them. I wish I can find out more; but they tell me to keep my mouth shut and do my job." She replied to Benson.

Just as they were finishing up with the bloodwork. Ally comes back in to talk to Daniel. She had a worried look on her face.

"What's up? What happened?" He asked Shepard.

"Some poor hooker got murdered last night. She might not live far from here." She explained.

"Well, does your captain want us on the case?" He asked.

"Well, no he wants us on this case, but I am kind of curious." She told him.

"Well let's go then." Benson told Ally.

As soon as Daniel got done with the bloodwork, they headed off to see the crime scene. A few minutes later they were at the crime scene. Ally showed the cops her badge and let the cops know Benson was with her. The hooker's body was covered up as people were trying to get a look at what the body looked like. When Ally and Daniel got close to the body they asked to see the body. The coroner pulled off the sheet of the body and it wasn't mauled. But it looked like it was drained of its blood.

"Jesus Christ! What the fuck! Who would do such a thing to this woman?" she asked in disgust.

Daniel just stood there trying to figure out how the blood could be drained. *"Their look at her neck. There are two holes in her neck."* He pointed to the holes.

Ally looked at what he was pointing at.

"It doesn't look like it was a vampire because the holes are not together and not even. They look like needles that punctured the neck. He looked over the body. *"Is this body going to the city morgue?"* He asked one of the coroners.

The coroner just nodded his head yes. The coroner picked up the body and put it in the back of the van to head to the morgue. After a forty-five-minute drive to the city morgue, Benson and Shepard got out of the car and went to the building to see what they could find out more information about the victim. Once they filled out the paperwork, they went to the back to find the head doctor to see what clues they could come up with about the unnamed hooker. Once they opened the swinging door, they saw the doctor about to do the autopsy on her. *"May I help you folks?"* She asked.

"NYPD ma'am." Ally showed the doctor her badge.

Benson stood next to her, *"We need to know about this hooker and why she was drained of her blood."* She told the doctor.

"I see and who is this gentleman with you?" The doctor asked Ally.

Before she could answer Daniel replied, *"I'm with a different department ma'am. Top secret."*

The doctor looked confused and announced, *"Okay then. I was just about to do the autopsy on this hooker. If you want to see?"* She told them both.

They both walked to the table. Benson started getting cravings because of the smell of bodies and blood so, he went to his pocket to get his blood gun out to shoot it in his neck. When they reached the table, the doctor opened up the sheets to uncover the body. The doctor was beginning the autopsy. *"Here we have an unknown Hispanic female maybe in her mid to her late twenties about five- feet six. One- hundred thirty pounds. The victim seems to have her blood drained out completely. I see two holes on the right side of her neck. Hmm, it looks like something like a needle or tube entered her neck. But that is impossible. Needles can't do that to this woman. Unless it was a machine that did it?"* Noted the doctor.

"May I see the neck please?" Benson asked the doctor.

The doctor nodded her head yes. Daniel walked around to see the neck. Daniel started to look at the neck. *"Hmm this is not vampire. It has to be like some kind of tube. The holes are not even, and these ones are a bit bigger."* He noted.

"How do you know it is not vampires? Vampires are not real. You watch one too many movies." The doctor told Benson.

Daniel picked up his head and took off his sunglasses. He turned his head to the doctor and showed her his red eyes and teeth. *"How about now?"* He asked her.

The doctor freaked out and screamed as she ran out of the room.

"Was that really necessary Daniel?" Shepard asked him.

"She needed to be warned about the vampires. This one is not turning because she would have turned by now." He said.

"I still don't believe you." She told him.

Benson stopped what he was doing to show Ally the difference between a bite and needle mark. He saw a. Pepsi Zero Sugar on the doctor's desk. He walked to the doctor's desk, took the can, and took a bite of it with his vampire teeth.

"I forgot you people like soda. Gross, but look here my marks are even and small. Now let us find some needles to see if I am right." He assured her. As they are searching the room for needles or some tubes.

They found a few of them. They found one tube that fit the holes in the neck.

"Fucking told you. Don't ever doubt me again!" He told Shepard.

"Okay. I'm sorry, but now next question? How in the fuck did blood come out quick? Tubes don't drain them quick unless they have a machine that does it or something?" She told him.

Just before Daniel could answer, she got a call on her cell and so did he. After a few minutes on their cell phones, they turned to each other.

"Was your call the same thing as mine?" She asked.

"You mean someone got arrested for selling vampir?" He replied.

"Yep, let's go!" They both agreed, at the same time.

Before they could leave Benson had to find the doctor so he could apologize. Once he found the doctor's office, he knocked on the door to see if he could come in. Nothing, no answer, so he tried the doorknob. It was unlocked, so he let himself in.

"Hello? Doctor? I just came in here to apologize. And to let you know we are leaving." He said.

No response. Then he hears a noise coming from the bathroom. He takes out one of his daggers just in case she is in trouble. He went to the bathroom door to see if he could come in. He knocked.

"Hello! Doctor? Is everything okay?" He asked. All he could hear was some whimpers on the other side. He knocked again and then the whimpers stopped. *"What the hell is she doing?"* he asked himself.

Just then her hand comes out of the door, and she punches him and grabs Daniel by the neck. He tries to move his head to see the hole on the door. Once he did, the look on his face was shocked, she had turned into one of the minions when she took the drug V.

"DAYWALKER!" She screamed.

Benson, with all of his strength, pushed her towards the door so it could break. It did with her on top of him with force so much he dropped his dagger. He tried to look for something sharp to kill her with. *"Get off me you ugly bitch!"* He told her. As she was trying to bite Daniel's head off, but then here comes Ally.

She busted open the door. *"Ah shit!"* Ally noted.

The doctor stopped doing what she was doing to Daniel and turned her focus on Ally. *"More fresh blood!"* She replied as she began running towards Shepard.

Ally tried to get her gun, but Benson beat her to the punch. He threw his dagger at the vampire doctor.

Once he threw his dagger at her, she was killed quick as she exploded, blood spilled all over the place. Even on Ally. *"Are you okay?"* Benson asked her as he tried not to laugh.

"You know in college, I only did a girl once. Just once and she never spilled her juices on me. But this one. Oh my God! I turned her on I guess." She replied.

Daniel laughed at her joke.

"Not funny. I have to go home and change." she noted.

"Well, I hope you live in the Bronx. We have no time. It will be daylight soon and the sun will kill off those pricks or they will hide." He told her.

"But I'm sticky and smell like blood and shit." Shepard complained.

"Well congratulations. You popped your cherry. I have been doing it for almost a hundred years and I have gotten blood, shit, piss, and food on me when I started out. I even had a dick and balls on me when I shot and blew up a minion." He told her. They both paused for a minute then he said. *"Fine! Go home and change but meet me after in Jersey for some pie."* He told her.

She agreed and she left the back of the building while Benson went out of the window of the doctor's office.

Chapter Nine

Ally was heading to her apartment to change. Daniel went ahead and went to the Bronx to see who got infected by the drug V. While he was heading for the hour and a half drive, he decided to make some calls. His first call was to Doctor Andrea Lovato.

"Hello?" She answered.

"Doctor, have you looked up anything on this Doctor Justin Drake?" Benson asked.

"You know what, I have checked every doctor listing from New York and nothing. Not even around the world. That is weird to me because I know every doctor. I have met them all except this one." She told him.

"Well shit, if we find out who he is then we can end this. He is the one who's blood is making the drugs. Are you telling me he is invisible? What about the Invictus Society? Do they know who he is?" He asked.

"No, they have no clue either, but they are still working on it." She told him.

"Fuck me! Okay thanks Andrea. Have you heard from Robert and helped him?" He asked.

"I did help him. I gave him some meds for the migraines, but last I heard he was going on a two-week vacation." She replied.

"Hmm, two-week vacation? That doesn't sound like him. He likes to work on the weapons or come up with new ones. Did he say where he was going?" He asked.

"Yeah, he mentioned he was going to Colorado to see family," replied Andrea.

"Okay. I'll see him in two weeks then. I'm off to the Bronx. We have our first person to use the drug v. I will tell the Society now. Thank you. Doctor, have a good night," replied Daniel. They both hung up the phone. He urgently called the Invictus Society.

"Any news Benson?" asked April.

"Yes, as a matter of fact, the drug vampir has hit. Someone is selling it in the Bronx. I'm heading there now. Shepard went to change. The morgue doctor took the drug and turned. I had to do what I had to do." He told her.

"Understood. We are still looking at who this Dr. Justin Drake fellow is. We will keep you updated. Good luck." She hung up the phone. Then Benson called one more person.

Ring

Ring

Ring

Ring

"You have reached the voicemail of Robert Herrera. Please leave your message after the beep."

"Fucker!" Benson replied. He reached his destination in the Bronx. He found what he was looking for by the cops lights and he saw Captain Benjamin.

"William." Daniel called out to him.

The captain waved him to cross the police tape to see what happened. *"Where's Shepard?"* He asked him.

"Had to shower. We ran into trouble. Had splats of blood on her and her face. So, she is going to meet me in Jersey. I can catch her up to speed. What do we got here?" He asked.

"Female in her early forties white, has tattoos, a few piercings, blue eyes, and with brunette hair. She's the drug dealer. Her name is Naya Grimes, but she goes by White Rhino," added Benjamin.

"Has she turned yet? Where are the drugs?" Daniel asked.

"No, she hasn't turned yet. Not that I know of. The drugs. He pointed to the drugs *There are still some left. We will take it and put it away for evidence. We will take her to the station now if you want to talk to her?"* the captain asked.

"Yeah, that would be great. Call Ally and let her know. I'll head to the Bronx police department now," reported Benson.

As the crowd was walking away, the police were wrapping up everything. Benson thought it was a clever idea to check her apartment. He walked into Naya's apartment, and he noticed how clean it was. *"Not bad for a dealer. I thought they had dirty houses?"* He said to himself.

After checking out every room he thought he would check her bedroom. Once he opened the door, the look of horror on his face was shocking. Blood and lumps of rotten meat were all over the place. He even found some of the drugs with dirty syringes. Then a note caught his eye.

Dr. Drake is amazing. He knows what he is doing. His cock is good and the way he fucks me makes me so wet. He promised to take me away from this place. I told him I would sell each and every ounce of his drugs just to be with him. I

love him and I want to be with him, and I would do anything to be with him t.t.f.n. with love Misses Naya Drake.

After reading the note, he now knew he had to talk to and see Drake. What was in his drugs. Daniel reached for his phone to call Ally. After a few rings she picked up.

"You find anything in the Bronx?" She asked him.

"Yes, meet me at Bronx police station. Hurry, they have someone, and I want to interview her. I'm heading there now. See you soon." Benson hung up on her and called the Society.

"Yes, Daniel any news?" Gina asked on the other line.

"Yes, the police have someone in custody. I'm going to head there now. I'll report back if anything shows up." He told Gina. Then ended the call. He was about to leave when he heard a familiar voice in the darkness.

"You know you look good with the shave and a haircut." The voice announced.

"That voice? is that you Amaya?" asked Benson He was turning around and sure enough it was Amaya as she was hiding in the bedroom. She walked towards the little lamp that was showing some light.

"What the hell are you doing here?" Daniel asked. He grabbed his gun from the back of his pants.

"I followed you. I have been since the morgue." She confessed to him as she walked closer to Benson.

"Why? So, you can tell those two dead fucks. I should call your grandmother and send you back to her." He threatened her.

"Look, I work for an organization called the Sacred Fire. We investigate cases that involve the paranormal and other odd things. Once we heard about the vampires and their drugs, we had to get involved." She told Benson.

"But why now? Why come to us now?" He asked.

"Because we too have a goal and that is to stop these fucks from taking over the world. We tried to make a deal with the Invictus Society, but they told us no and not to get involved. We are all over the world. As a matter of fact, we are watching a LAPD Detective named Angel De La Cruz. We see something in him. Like I see something in you." She explained to him.

"So, let me get this straight you're with a secret organization? You are watching another person, and you are helping me? Do you work for a Russian guy who calls himself Dock?" Benson asked Amaya.

"No, but it looks like he is helping you." She told him. They were face to face. They both could tell they were starting to have feelings for one another. She was about to kiss him again, but then he stopped her.

"Now is not the time. I know you have feelings for me. I can sense it, but it is not the time. I have to complete this case, kill off Koi and Rebekah, find this Dr. Drake, and end this nightmare." Daniel told her.

Amaya backed off a bit. She had a look of heartbreak in her eyes. She was crushed.

He was going to tell her something else, but then his phone rang. He looked to see who it was. It was Dock. When he looked back up; Amaya was gone.

"Enough of this batman disappearing act bullshit." He said out loud. He answered the phone *"What's up Dock?"* He asked.

"I'm in New York. I brought backup and we are on standby, have you found anything?" Stated Dock.

"As a matter of fact, I have. I know whose blood it is. Some guy named Dr. Justin Drake. The only problem is, we don't know who he is or what kind of doctor he is. I'm about to talk to someone in custody in the Bronx." Benson replied.

"Good, keep me updated. We will help you out for the favor you gave us overseas. We will find out who this doctor is. Good luck with your mission." Then they hanged up the phone.

Daniel was leaving for the police station. He took the note with him to talk to Naya. Benson was headed to the Bronx police station. He googled it as it was a twenty-minute drive. After a twenty-minute drive he arrived at the station where Ally and Capt. William were outside waiting for him.

"What took you so long? Having us to wait for you in this damn cold?" Shepard told him.

"I was looking for proof. And some leads. I found this note." He reported to them as he was handed the note to them. *"Maybe we can use this to get her to talk. I have a plan,"* added Benson.

After going over the plan and agreeing to it. Benson and Shepard were ready to interrogate the prisoner. After a few minutes, the police came and got Naya and put her in the room where it was barely lit. Ally was waiting for her kept looking at her file.

"You must be Naya Grimes also known as White Rhino. Please sit down." Ally told her.

The police put the cuffs on the cuff hook. Then the cops left the room leaving Ally and Naya alone.

"Let's see you got a long rap sheet. It started when you were ten and went on until now. You are being charged with illegal drugs. The new drug called Vampir do you want to tell me about it?" She asked Naya.

She didn't say anything.

"What is this drug? and who is the supplier?" Shepard explained. Still Grimes wouldn't say anything.

"You know they are right. You do look like a rhino. Talk to me girl to girl." Ally insulted her.

Then after a few minutes Ally didn't get a word from her as Ally was leaving, she finally said something.

"Can I leave now. Since you got nothing on me?" She asked Shepard.

"I'm done with you, but he's not." She told her.

The door closed, the lights turned on, and Daniel was behind her, He slammed her, head on the metal desk.

"She was nice to you, but I won't be! Now talk druggie bitch!" Demanded

Benson as he sat down.

"My husband told me about you. You're the day walker. If you were to catch me, I couldn't talk to you." She told him.

"So, you know who Drake is and what he looks like?" He asked.

"Yes, but I won't say anything so you might as well take me to my cell. So, I can go to court." She told Benson.

"Oh, honey it's going to be much worse with that." He told Naya.

He then grabbed his chair and put it against the door so no one could get in. From the other side of the window, Capt. Benjamin, Ally, and the rest of the police officers were running to open the door. They were banging on the door. Daniel threw her on the floor so hard that the cuffs broke on the table.

"WHO THE FUCK IS HE AND WHERE IS HE?" Benson yelled at her while choking her out.

"Okay, okay, I will tell you." She agreed as he grabbed another chair to put on her throat to get information. *"NOW TALK BITCH!"* He ordered her.

He is tall and black. He is not a doctor. I don't know what he does. All I know he dresses nice and very good looking." She tells Benson.

Daniel had to think for a minute. *"Where is the blood coming from?"* He asked *"I don't know. He just gave me a few crates and I sold them. Well, I sold half of it, and I kept some for myself."* She confessed after a minute.

"Names! Give me the names of the people you sold it to!" Benson demanded Grimes.

She didn't say anything because she was struggling to breathe. Then Daniel notices a piercing on the middle of her nose. *"You know what I really hate? Those fucking septum piercings. You all look like a goddamn bull. I want to get a red blanket and say oley."* He confessed to her, then he leaned closer to her with the chair, and he grabbed the piercing.

"You want to tell me anything else? Since you are so in love with him?" He asked her. She didn't say anything as she was still struggling to breathe. Then Daniel noted. *"You know it is a pretty piercing. Too bad it's got to go."* Benson ripped it and blood started to squirt everywhere.

He got off the chair and went to the door to get the other chair so the police could open the door up. As soon the door was unlocked, the guards opened the door to check on her, they picked her up and they rushed her to the emergency room.

"Was that necessary? What the fuck did you do?" Shepard asked Daniel.

"I got information we needed since she wasn't talking to you. I had no choice." Benson told Ally.

"Off to Jersey I'm hungry for some pie." He said.

"Do what you want to do. I'm going to go home." Ally replied rudely.

After the argument they both left. Daniel headed straight to New Jersey while Ally headed home.

Chapter Ten

O nce Daniel made it to Jersey, he headed to the diner to eat. On the way there he had flashbacks. New Jersey, 1920. After a great date with Rebecca, Daniel and she went to the Diner to meet her father, Quinn O' Conner. *"I'm nervous about meeting your dad. What happens if he doesn't like me, or he punches me?"* Daniel asked Rebecca.

"Everything will be okay babe." She assured him. *"He will like you, you're the first boyfriend that treats me good. The rest don't count because I was in school."*

"Well, that makes me feel a hell of a lot better. Oh shit! I forgot something in the car. Go inside and meet your dad. I will be there in a minute." Benson told her.

Rebecca did what was asked and went inside. Daniel reached inside of his jacket pocket and pulled out a box. He opened it up and there was a very nice diamond ring. *"Okay Mister O'Conner. I hope you like me because I love your daughter and want you to give me your blessing to marry her."* Benson practiced his speech nervously.

After that, he closed the box and put it inside his pocket, he then went inside the diner where he saw Rebecca waving him over to meet her dad. When the flashback was over, he was at the parking lot at the diner. He got out of his car and locked it up. He then went inside to sit at his usual spot where Debbie began walking towards him.

"Hey Benson. The same thing?" She asked.

"Yes, and maybe some coffee. It has been too long since I had a hot cup of coffee." He told her.

The look on Debbie's face went from happy to shock because Daniel never drinks coffee. After a few minutes Debbie came back with his usual and he finally got to relax after a rough night. After he got done with his food he got up and was leaving but, Debbie noticed something odd about him.

"Sit down. Something is off about you What is wrong?" She asked him.

After wiping his face with both hands, he finally confessed.

"The drug has hit. I had to kill a morgue doctor. I do not know where the source is coming from. This is the hardest son of a bitch case I have ever done. I don't know where the blood is coming from?" Benson told Debbie.

She placed her hand on Daniel's shoulder and replied, *"You are a good half human, half vampire, a great detective, and a good father who is trying to wake up his daughter. You are like my own son. What's up with the shave and a haircut? You liking somebody? Was it that woman you were with a few nights ago?"* Debbie asked as she smiled at Daniel.

He giggled and replied, *"No it is someone new. I can tell she likes me. I can sense it in her like I did a long time ago when I first met Rebecca. Listen, if I were you, I would close shop for the night. I would close now just to be safe."*

Debbie had known Daniel for many years, and she knew that if he had told her something it was in her best interest to do whatever it was, he suggested. *"Let me clean up and I'll close it down."* She told Daniel, giving him a warm smile before walking away.

Benson went outside while he waited for Debbie and the cook to leave. After a few minutes they all went their own ways. Daniel was headed to the New York cemetery even though it was closed so he could talk to Rebecca. After an hour-long drive, he made it to the cemetery and went to Rebecca's grave. He took off his sunglasses and started talking.

"Hey honey. I know it has been a minute since I have been here, but I'm having trouble with this case. I know you can hear me. I'm stuck, I only have a few more weeks before the world goes to shit. I have never had a case this big and it fucking sucks. I just wish I can see you, your dad, and my family to get advice."

All of a sudden, he heard whispers. It sounded like everyone that passed on was giving him good advice. He then saw a bright light coming towards him. Once the light was beginning to dimmer, Benson was shocked. He could see Rebecca's spirit. She looked young and was in a long white dress. Her hair was still fire red when they met. Her eyes had more sparkle than ever before.

"I missed you too." She announced in her thick Irish accent.

"I can't do this anymore. The only reason I keep going is because of Leah." He told her.

"I know you don't want to do it anymore, but you must keep fighting the good fight. Everyone you love depends on you. Soon you will see them, just say their names and they will be there. Now get up and get on your feet before I kick your arse. Keep fighting." She told him. Before he could get up on his feet, she convinced him. *"By the way. I like that woman. Please have sex with her. You need someone. I will see you soon, we love you."*

He grinned as he left the cemetery. Once he got into his car it stalled. Daniel reached into his shirt to grab something on his neck. He moved his medallion and reached for what he was searching for. It was Benson's wedding ring which was another good luck charm.

"Okay Rebecca! I'll do what you ask." He told her.

He then tried to start his car again. This time there was no stalling.

October 15th. After a few days of no movement from Koi or Rebekah, or Drake, Daniel and Ally kept hearing about murders that involved dead prostitutes or with women. They had the same M.O. They found the same thing, holes in their necks and blood completely gone. They have not turned into vampires yet.

"No turning into vampires, no nothing. Either we have a vampire wannabe or just a sick tormented killer on our hands." Ally told Daniel.

"I don't know, but I wish Robert was here. He would find out. Not even Doctor Lovato can figure out what is happening." He told her.

Shepard asked Benson, *"Well what do you want to do?"*

He paused for a few minutes and explained, *"Well I figured we could see if someone has seen anything or if there are any cameras outside where the attacks have happened."* He told her.

She agreed to Benson's idea. They were both heading their separate ways. Ally to her office at the NYPD and Daniel heading to the Invictus Society. Benson arrived at the Invictus Society building where he went and saw a computer hacker named Tom Croft.

"Hey Tom, do you have a minute?" asked Benson. "

For you. I've got five. What's up?" Tom asked. Croft was in his early thirties, about six five, bald and wears glasses. Croft was turning down his music on his phone.

"I have a case maybe you can help on. Women and prostitutes. They haven't turned into vampires, they have just been having their blood drained out of their bodies. I was wondering if you could hack into the city video cameras to see who it is because they just drain the blood and leave." He told Croft.

Before Tom could answer there was a voice on the intercom. **"Daniel Benson please report to the cells. Repeat, Daniel Benson please report to the cells."**

"Fuck!" He said as he began to run, he told Tom, *"Get it done!"* Benson was hauling ass to the cells where they keep Akasha's stone body. When he reached the elevator doors, he hit the button to go down to the basement cells. Once the elevator dinged and the doors opened, he ran to the cell where Akasha's cell was at. There were a lot of guards pointing their guns up and pointed at the stone body.

"What is going on here?" asked Daniel.

"For the last few days, we have seen blood coming out of her mouth. She keeps moving." One of the guards told him. Daniel pushed the guards out of the way to see. When he stopped, he motioned the guards to put their weapons down as he got close to Akasha and spoke. *"Who's feeding you? It hasn't been a thousand years yet. Do You know who Drake is? It won't matter who he is. It will matter when you are not stone anymore, and I kill you again with Drake and those other two fuckers. Once I get my daughter back, it will be all over. But in the meantime, these guards will watch over you and if you move again, they will crush you. TRY ME CUNT!"* Benson told her. He was angry, his eyes

were red fire, and his fangs showed that he bit his mouth by mistake.

"If this big bitch moves then you have my permission to smash her to little pieces." Benson told the guards. They all nodded yes to Daniel as he left. Then he headed back up to the elevator, he hit the button, then his phone rang. He looked at his phone and it was the doctor.

"Yes Andrea." He replied, still trying to calm down.

"You better get to your daughter's room. She moved her eyes and her finger." She told him. Benson with excitement was waiting for the elevator doors to open. A few seconds later the elevator doors dinged, and the doors opened. Daniel rushed to the elevator to push the button to see Leah. A few seconds later Benson made it to his daughter's room where Doctor Lovato and her nurse Carla was in there.

"What happened? Is she still active?" Benson asked Lovato.

"Yes, Carla was just checking her vitals and noticed her eyes were moving. So, she came and got me. I started to hold Leah's hand, and she squeezed it. I want to see if she can do it again, but with you here Daniel." She told him.

"Okay let's do this." He told her as he got close to his daughter's bed, he sat down, and he started to hold her hand hoping she could squeeze his hand. After a few minutes nothing happened. So, he tried talking to her to see if that could work, he got up from his chair and spoke.

"Hey honey, it is me, your daddy. I heard your eyes moved and you squeezed a hand. That's great, can you squeeze my hand? Let me know that everything will be okay." Benson told his daughter. A few minutes went by and nothing. After trying to

squeeze his hand Daniel gave up. He bent over and was going to kiss her forehead. Leah spat at him right in the face.

He was shocked about what happened to him. He didn't know what to do. He turned to see the doctor and the nurse. They were shocked as well.

"Please tell me that is part of her condition? If not, then that bitch did it." He told Lovato.

"Well yes and no. I have heard cases about that, but this was a first. They usually respond to voices they know, not to spit at them. I'm so sorry, but I think you need to go." She told him.

Benson just ignored her, and he went back to his seat and sat down. He stared at Leah. His phone was ringing but he kept ignoring it till the Invictus Society member Gina had to go to his daughter's room to find him.

"Hey, we have been looking for you. We need you to scope out Koi and Rebekah. Find out what they are doing and see if they have met up with Dr. Drake." She told him.

"Kiss my ass! I'm not going. I'm going to stay here by my daughter's side and wait for her to wake up." He told Gina.

"I don't care! The boss says we need you. So, get Ally and go. We need to end this nightmare." She ordered him.

"No, you just want me to end this nightmare. I'm out there risky my life and yet the boss says he will kill me and end my daughter's life. If the boss was here and had balls, he would tell me in front of my fucking face. But he is being a pussy ass bitch!" Benson angrily told Gina.

Before he could say another word, he got a call on his phone from Ally.

"Let me guess, they called you so we can spy on those two fucks, right?"

"Yes, I'm across from their club. I got food, see you soon."

After the phone call he left Leah's room to head out. With Gina behind him, He stops and turns around. Looks at Gina and spoke.

"If anything happens to my daughter, I swear I will end your boss and end the Invictus Society as well." He told her.

She just nodded yes and watched Daniel leave the building. He went to go see Ally so they could spy on Koi and Rebecka. They needed to figure out who Dr. Drake was.

Benson and Shepard met up at The Nipple Clamps there was a little Chinese restaurant across from the club. The Nipple Clamps was being remodeled but was still open to the public. Ally was sitting in her car eating some Chinese food while Benson opened her door to get in. It been raining all day, and it had continued in the night.

"Shit, I hate this fucking weather. These assholes control the weather." Benson reported to Ally as she handed him some noodles to eat. He grabbed the noodles and started to eat.

"Did you find anything on the killer?" She asked him.

"No. But we have a computer geek who is going to help us. He has hacked all the city cameras so hopefully we can find out who it is." He confessed to her. A few hours later, a limo pulls up at the club. Ally and Daniel were hoping it was Koi and Rebekah. When the limousine driver opened the door, it was them and some guests. They were all holding umbrellas.

"Shit! I don't know if any of the other people are Drake." Observed Benson *"I have to find out. Give me the binoculars."*

"What are you going to do?" She questioned him.

"You see that apartment building? It looks across from the office of the club. I'm sure that is where they are going. That is

where I would go to have a private party." Replied Benson. *"Let me know if anything happens."*

Shepard nodded yes. Benson went outside in the cold rainy weather. *"Well at least I don't burn like the rest."*

He knew he could get water on him but not too much because it would burn. One of the many weaknesses of being a half human half vampire. He ran as fast as he could and covered up as much as he could. Once outside the building he was going to try to find an empty apartment building to match the same floor as the office building to the club. After reaching the top floor and using his aura, he found an empty apartment. He climbed on the outside wall to unlocked the window. He went inside and he found a spot where the office windows are at.

"Come on! Where are you at? Come to papa." He said out loud.

After a few minutes Koi, Rebekah and their three guests walked in. From what Daniel saw with the binoculars, they were partying and dancing. Rebekah took her gentleman friend to the other room while Koi stayed with the other two one male and one female in the office. Benson was focusing on everything, before he can sets his sights on Koi and his guest he paused as what he saw. Daniel saw the female go down on Koi and then a second later the male did too.

"Well, I'll be damn." He was shocked. Koi didn't seem like the type to go both ways.

And then he stayed there spying on Koi. He was about to leave but then one of his Dhampir sense kicked in to tell him to stay. So, he went back to the window with the binoculars and just looked at them all. Then all of a sudden, the lights went out in the office then back on. The party guest bodies were dead on the ground. Benson couldn't find Koi till he moved the binoculars, and there was Koi and Rebekah being held by their throats by an unknown person. Wearing all black Trent coat, hat and this person was huge. Koi and Rebekah were naked, and they seemed to be scared of this person as they were burning up as well in the rain. The unknown figure had both of them at the edge of the open office building dangling by their throats. Benson can't see the figures face as it is covered.

Chapter Eleven

"*S hit! I wish I knew what that person was saying to them. They look scared as fuck.*" Benson told himself. After a few minutes the figure pulled Koi and Rebekah back inside from being dangled by their throats at the edge of the building. Daniel could now leave but he wanted to know who that figure was. When he went back to the binoculars, the figure must have sensed Benson across the street. It was a wicked sense of Déjà Vu. The figure pointed at Daniel.

"*What the fuck? no fucking way! It can't be! Please tell me that my nightmare is not coming true?*" Benson panicked as he tried to get up on his feet to leave the building. He opened the window and jumped. Once he landed on his feet and he ran to the car as quickly he could.

"*What happened in there?*" She told him. "*Just go! Drive Ally! Drive now!*" *He* screamed at her. Before she could say anything, the hooded figure landed on top of Ally's car, he then pointed his finger at Daniel again.

"*FUCKING GO ALLY!*" Benson yelled at her. She started up her car and started to take off; the hooded figure was still on the hood of the car. Shepard was driving till Daniel seen a light post near-by.

"Aim for the light post kill this motherfucker!" He demanded Shepard.

"Are you fucking crazy? That will hurt both of us." She refused.

He just ignored her and took the wheel of the car. He put his foot on top of Ally's foot to speed up the car. Once the hooded figure saw what Benson was doing, he flew back up in the sky like superman. They both saw the light post, but it was too late to stop the car. The car hit the light pole hard. The doors opened and Shepard and Benson climbed out uninjured, they just had some scratches and bruising. The car was totaled. Smoke was coming out of the engine and then the light pole fell down on the car, right in the middle of it. They were both lucky they didn't get killed. The rain started to come down heavily. Daniel looked up at the sky and his skin began to burn.

"What the fuck is wrong with you? We could have been killed you stupid fuck. I wish I never teamed up with you! I wish I could have arrested you. Who's going to pay for my car? Are you going to pay for my car? Or is that goddamn Club you are in? Are they going to pay for it?" She was furious and didn't hold anything back.

Daniel completely ignored her and walked to his loft in the rain. *"FUCK YOU DANIEL BENSON!"* Shepard yelled to him.

October 20th. Twelve days 'till Halloween and Daniel has been M.I.A. for five days. Since the night he freaked out over the hooded figure.

Meanwhile more killings of prostitutes and women with the same M.O. Blood is drained but no new vampires. The Invictus Society and Ally had no choice but to keep working on the case 'till Benson came back. The meeting continued, along with Doctor Lovato, Croft, and Herrera on what they could figure out what they could do.

"Has anyone tried calling Benson or has been to his loft?" April asked.

Everyone nodded no.

"I'm still pissed at him for wrecking my car!" Ally told everyone.

"Well, you better apologize to him because we need him. From what I've heard, the basement jail cell is getting crazier with that thing down there." Gina told everyone.

"And his daughter is more active. The more this thing moves, the more his daughter moves." Lovato replied. Herrera stood up and left without saying a word.

"You know since he came back from his vacation, he is still acting like a dickhead. I wonder what his problem is." Carla mentioned it to the doctor. They both giggled then went back to pay attention to the meeting. While everyone was wondering where Daniel was. The big screen that all of their clues on went black, the boss face then appeared on the screen.

"Where in the hell is Benson? He should have been here!" He told everyone.

"We don't know. Ally mentioned something that happened to him. And he has been M.I.A. He freaked out over someone and hasn't been the same since." Explained Gina.

"Well in that case, his daughter is gone and if he comes back, he is gone too." The boss announced.

"Wait! You can't do that! His daughter is finally moving. She is finally making progress. You can't do that!" Lovato cried to him.

The boss didn't say anything for a few minutes then confessed. "Fine! I'll give him one more chance. You have forty-eight hours to find him. If you know where he lives, go there first. If he's not there then go to where he hangs out. If you don't find him, I'm pulling the plug on his kid, and I will kill him personally!" He told everyone.

The screen went back to normal. Everyone just looked at one another hoping for answers. They didn't know where he lived. It was just an unknown loft in the city.

"Well, when does Ally start?" April asked as she turned her head at Shepard.

"Wait, why me? Why do I have to look for him?" she argued with April.

"Because it's your job to detect. Do what you need to do. Get him food, get him a new gun, suck his cock! Anything because if not, the world will go to hell." April plead with Ally.

"Fine I'll start in New Jersey. He goes to a diner there for pie." She told them.

"You better get on it then. The clock is ticking his life and his daughter's life depends on it." Gina warned.

By the time Ally saw Robert to see about a new gun and measured for a body suit for the project Black Thunder it was almost the evening time before she hit the road. Good thing she works for the zombie squad because she would be tired at this point, after getting a cup of coffee. Took the hour drive up there; the weather at this point is still shitty just cold and windy but no rain for once. When she got to New Jersey she went to the diner, and it was only Debbie that was working, and she saw Shepard walking into the diner and spoke.

"Hey, you're Ally, right? The one who came with Daniel that night?"

"Yes, has he been here? We are looking for him." She told her.

"Just a few days ago. He mentioned his nightmare had come true and explained he needed to hide. I don't know what he was talking about. I just thought he was acting strange, but he never does. He didn't even get his usual order. he really ate pie." Debbie told Shepard.

"Do you know where to find him? Has he ever given you an address for a Grub hub or Door dash delivery?" Shepard asked Debbie.

"Oh no. He never delivered. He would always make the hour drive, even when we were on lockdown. He even kept the diner going due to the lockdown a few years ago. I wish I could help you out more, but I can't." Debbie told her.

After using the diner bathroom to pee and to get a coffee to go. Ally was back on the road headed back to New York to figure out how to find Benson. She had to find him to finish this case.

After arriving back to the city, Ally thought it would be a good idea to head to The Nipple Clamps in Hell's Kitchen. Maybe she could find the dancer that Benson was talking to when the club blew up. The Nipple Clamps were done with the remodeling of the building. From the outside, people were standing outside in the cold waiting to get in. Ally parked her car then walked up to the bouncer. She took her badge from around her neck to showed the bouncer to let him know she's NYPD.

The people outside were mad and grumbled at Shepard as she walked inside. She noticed it was way different than before.

Darker red lights, everywhere in the club was jammed packed with dancers and a DJ. The stripper poles where completely gone, and the band was gone. Just a dance floor and a bar.

"What the fuck happened to this place? It's more like a goth vampire club." She mumbled under her breath as she walked towards the bartender.

A few men were calling her pet names and whistling at her. One of them yelled to her, *"Hey officer! You can arrest me anytime. Just watch out for my big ol' weapon between my legs. It might go off once you touch it."*

The rest of the guys laughed and continued drinking their beers. Ally just ignored them as she walked past them and right up to the bar where the bartender was. She stood at the bar table and whistled at the bartender to get his attention.

He turned around and she flashed her badge at him.

"What can I help you with officer?" He asked Shepard.

"Looking for a dancer. I need to question her." She answered.

"Who is the dancer? We got lots of them. Some of them are servers and bartenders as well." He mentioned it to her.

"Can I just go look in the back?" She asked.

"Not without a warrant bitch! What are you going to do? Arrest me?" He laughed at her.

"Fine, I'll leave and come back with a warrant. Then I'll arrest you for being an asshole." She threatened him.

The bartender just laughed at her.

The guys who were looking at Ally were still giving her shit. One of them joked, *"Hey baby let's go in the back and I'll show you my .357 magnum. It's cocked, locked, and ready to unload."* He untastefully told Ally.

Suddenly, she had an idea. She went back to one of the guys and asked flirtatiously, *"Do you know what? I'll take that offer big boy. I'm horny as fuck. Let's go fuck in the back. I'll suck your cock so good your soul will leave."*

Then the other guys were egging him on to go so, he stood up and he and Ally were heading to the alley while they were all cheering.

After a few minutes, it was raining again so Shepard and the guy went into the back of the alley. to what the guy is thinking that they are going to have sex.

"Alright big boy. Take off your pants and let me see it." She told him.

The guy did what he was told. He took off his pants, exposing his somewhat cock.

Ally looking confused she tilted her head from side to side thinking it would be huge. Then she started to giggle and laugh at the dude. *"Oh my god! My pinky is bigger than that!"* She insulted him.

The dude got pissed and was going to get Ally one way or another to do it with her. As he was going to get her with his pants all the way down to his ankles, he didn't know that Shepard had a taser gun behind her. Once he got close to her and grabbed her; she zapped him with the taser knocking him out cold and hitting the cement like a sack of potatoes.

"Thank you for that. I needed it." She told him. He was still cold, she then began to search his pockets to see if he had a pocketknife or credit card to open the back door of the club. luck would have it, he had a few pocketknives in his pocket. She gave him one more good kick for measure then she began to work on the door to unlock it. After a few minutes she broke

one knife, good thing she had another one. She finally got the back door opened. She went inside the club, pulled out her gun and started to head to the dressing room. She found a few locked doors and a janitor's room. She searched till she found a private door that said Santanico on it.

"Man, I hope this is the one that Benson is in love with." She told herself, then she checked the doorknob to see if it was unlocked and it was. She opened the rest of the door slowly with her gun still pointed out at everything in case something jumped out. Once she opened the door all the way, it was full of candles that were lit and a dresser mirror for her to do her makeup along with her clothes to change in and out of. Ally saw the dresser mirror door and she holstered her gun. She opened the door to the dresser mirror. There was nothing but papers and pictures of Daniel Benson. Amaya was checking on him and on the Invictus Society. she reads one of the notes on Benson.

I have been checking on Daniel and the Invictus Society. they are on a mission to kill off the vampires one by one. My grandma was right he is a good-looking guy I just wish he would lose the John Wick look. I must tell Sacred Fire and tell them about the mission.

"Huh sacred fire, Invictus Society, what is going to happen now? Werewolves? What the fuck!" Noted Ally then she read the second note.

I have been undercover for almost a month now. Koi and Rebekah don't know what I am or who I work for yet. If they found out what I'm trying to do, they would kill me. I must keep finding evidence and get out of here before it is too late.

Ally was about to close the drawer till she saw one more note.

I followed Daniel to his loft. I followed him all the way from New Jersey to New York. I have to see him. He must know that the Invictus Society are the bad people. I have to tell him.

Ally put away the note when she heard a noise coming from the bathroom. She quickly hid in the corner of the dark room. She took her gun out waiting for the door to open. Amaya walked out of the bathroom looking exhausted. She opened her drawer moving the notes and paper. Ally watched Amaya take out some pills and threw two of them in her mouth. She wasn't sure if they were drugs, she was taking, or just some aspirin. There was knock on her door and Shepard could hear a voice coming from the other side.

"Santanico, the Gods need your blessing, the blood party starts here in a few minutes." the unknown male voice told her.

"I will be there in a second." She told the male voice.

Amaya threw some makeup on her face. She was already beautiful, so she didn't need much. Amaya sensed that she was not alone in her room. *"I know you're here. I can sense you. Put down your weapon and tell me what you want cop!"* She told Shepard.

Ally did what Amya asked and came out of the dark and confronted Amaya. *"I'm looking for Benson. He has been missing for five days. We need him. Why are the Invictus bad people? And how did you know I was here?"* Shepard questioned her.

"First, I could smell your shampoo as soon as you walked in my room. Second, that leather jacket is way too noisy, and third, the notes were not in order and wet. Your hair was dripping

on them. If these people would have found out about me being undercover, they will kill me." She told Ally.

"I'm sorry but we need to find him. I had to break in the door because the bartender wouldn't let me see the dancers or whatever you girls call yourselves now. Can you help us find Benson? You followed him, please?" She begged Amaya.

Before Amaya could answer there was another knock on the door. Ally ran to the dark part of the room again and this time the door opened. It was the same unknown male voice as before, but this time he spoke in a different tone. *"It is time!"* He told Amaya.

Amaya nodded her head yes and stood up to leave. Before she walked out of the room, she gave Ally a quick stare. Her eyes suggested something, but Ally didn't know what she wanted her to do. Stay here and wait for her to return or just leave.

After a few minutes of waiting, Ally had to leave. She took the note with Benson's address on it then checked her watch. It was almost midnight. When she opened the door, she could still hear music. The club was busier than before so, this was the right time to leave the way she came in. She made it without notice, but once she reached the door, the music stopped. Then she stopped and checked her watch again. It was after midnight. She heard voices coming from the stage. She turned to look, and it was Amaya, Koi, and Rebekah. The lights turned red and all three of them had robes on. They began the ceremony.

"Ladies and gentlemen. Welcome to the new and improved Nipple Clamps. We have gathered everyone here tonight to celebrate the new owner of this establishment. Without him, we

would not have The Nipple Clamps as it is now. So, ladies and gentlemen please give it up for our new owner Dr. Justin Drake." Koi announced it to everyone.

Everyone began clapping. Amaya noticed Ally. She mouthed to Ally to leave but Ally couldn't read lips. She stayed to see what would happen next.

Chapter Twelve

The doctor finally spoke after the noise calmed *down.* "*Ladies and gentlemen. Welcome to the new and improved Nipple Clamps! I know it is not the same, but it is different, and I promise you will all have a good time.*" He told the people in the crowd.

Ally noticed he had an accent, but she still couldn't see what he looked like. His face and body were covered up with. Except his robe was a different color.

"*Now, since it is after midnight the party can really begin. Those people outside that have been waiting, they are inside now, but at a different side of the club. Where it is more of their style. Those who showed up early, you all are in for a special treat. Will my associates stand right next to me as I tell everyone this big announcement!*" He said.

Koi and Rebekah stood next to him, side by side and they took off their hoods exposing their faces. He then whispered something in both Koi and Rebekah's ears and they both walked away from Drake. Ally couldn't see where they went. She lost them in the darkness.

"*Ladies and gentlemen, say goodbye to your lives. Say goodbye to your normal lives. Say goodbye to everything you love and everyone you love. You belong to us now. We need more minions to hit this world. Say hello to your new life."* He announced to the crowd.

He took the hood part of the robe off and Ally still couldn't see what he looked like. She did see black ashy skin, with a shaved head. He held the drug V up in the air so the people could see it.

"With this new drug we have made, we shall rule the world. With three drops, you will not feel any more pain, no more sadness, just anger and hunger."

He then poured it in his eyes along with Koi and Rebekah. Then everyone else did the same. After a few minutes, the people in the crowd started to scream and holler in pain. Once the screaming stopped, Ally looked closer. The people had become vampires. Shepard had to get out of there, so she went to the back door of the club and left. The trucker then woke up dazed and confused. Shepard knocked him back out. She had to find Benson before it was too late. She ran to her car. Once she was in her car safe and sound, she looked for the note with Daniel's address on it. It read 2369 E 10th.

"That is not far from here. I have to go now." She told herself.

She was shaking off what happened. No one will believe her, not her captain, not the other officers. She hauled ass to Benson's loft without a moment too soon. Once she reached his loft, she parked her rented car across the street to his building. She entered the doors and began looking for his name on the mailbox, but she couldn't find it. She was about to give up when she saw a strange name on one of the mailbox. It read John Doe. The loft number read 503. She snapped her fingers and replied, *"Bingo."* She was then off to the fifth floor to see Benson.

Once the elevator doors opened to the fifth floor, she saw Daniel's door. She knocked a few times but nothing from the other side. She continued knocking on Benson's door till she remembered she had a pocketknife in her back pocket. With this door, it just needs to be jimmied with. Before she became a cop, she was a cat burglar with her dad. They were good at it until she was about twelve, her and her dad got caught. She did her time in juvie while her dad was still doing time up in Rykers. She still sees him from time to time. He encouraged her to become a cop to stop doing all this crime shit and do good with her life.

Once the door was unlocked, she walked right in. She took out her gun and started looking for Daniel. The loft was big. The more she scoped out his loft the more she became shocked about what his life was about. Nothing but weapons, daggers, and knives were on the wall. She even seen pictures of him with his family. One with his dad, his sister, his uncle and one with him and his sister. She was about to pick up the other picture of him and his family when she heard a voice behind her.

"What are you doing here?" Benson asked Shepard.

She turned around and it was Daniel who was walking like he had been drinking. He was holding a bottle of blood in one hand and a gun in the other.

"We have been looking for you Daniel. We got worried about you. Why are you holding that gun?" She asked him.

"This is my last chance. I tried hanging, poisoning, cutting myself, even jumping out the window and nothing. I heal up and come back a hundred percent. I can't jump out the window without landing on my feet." He told Ally as she got closer to him. He notices her doing so as he was taking steps back.

"Don't take another step or I'll do it and this time I won't come back." He warned her. He then went crazy. He threw the bottle of blood at Ally, almost hitting her. He then told her, *"Do you want to hear that sometimes I think about eating a bullet? Well, I do. I even have a special one for the occasion. It has a silver hollow point to make sure it blows the back of my goddamn heart out of my chest. Every single night I wake up and I think of a reason not to do it. Every single night."* He vented to Shepard.

He then put the gun down and wanted to break down, but he couldn't cry.

Ally thought it was safe to get close to him and just hug him. *"I know who Drake is. I know what he looks like. Your daughter keeps moving more we need you back."* She told him.

They both heard the door open, and it was Amaya. Shepard and Benson looked at one another then back to Amaya.

"You know. If you don't want people to find you or find out where you live change your name. John Doe was too easy. I would suggest B. Wayne." She told Benson.

"How did you find me? Did you follow her?" asked Benson as he pointed to Shepard.

"No, I followed you one night. I just didn't know what number and name till now. The reason I'm here to help you," she replied. *"Ally is right, they let the people in the club try the drug and that is how they turned. After that, they gave them the drug to spread out of the city. So now Koi, Rebekah and Drake have the drugs more and now they can tell their minions to sell more of the drug V; first Europe, then New York, then the world."* Amaya said.

Daniel just stood still for a minute then finally announced, *"Alright! I'm convinced, but first Shepard and I have to solve one case. Let me sober up and the three of us shall start tomorrow. This type D blood got me drunk last few days."* He told them.

As they were leaving, Benson stopped Amaya for minute, he took her hands and looked deep into her eyes he was still hesitant to kiss her. Then he kissed Amaya on the lips *"don't get killed."* He told her.

She just nodded her head, and she left too, leaving Daniel alone with his thoughts. As he was going through his phone that he ignored the last few days. He missed a few calls from headquarters from Thomas and from Dock, he thought he would call up dock because he never met up with him that night. Benson called Dock to explain to him what had happened, after a few rings Dock picked up his phone.

"What the hell happened to you? We all thought you were dead what the fuck happened to you?" He told dock.

"I'm sorry but you won't believe me, but my nightmare came true, and I had to go M.IA. I got drunk and tried to kill myself but I'm back and back to work, but still drunk." Daniel added.

"Hmm maybe I do believe you and maybe I don't, but we have been here waiting for you. We are ready to help you. Can you still meet up in an hour?" Dock asked.

"Yes, I'll see you in an hour." He replied.

As Benson was getting ready to see Dock, he needed to get sobered up, so he ate some food just to drive. After a few minutes he was starting to feel better, so he was heading out to see dock. As he was heading outside it started to snow. As Daniel was getting more pissed off because he knows the vampires are doing this he had to keep going before it was too late. Once he was at the hotel it had stopped snowing. Dock and his so-called company were at the New York Hilton hotel, and he remembers what hotel number they are at. He was ready to see Dock and find out what the fuck is going on with him and his plans to help Benson. After he took the elevator to the hotel suite, he found it and after a few knocks on the door Dock told him to come in. Once Benson went inside the room was barely lit and then he saw Dock sitting in the middle of the room.

"What's up Dock? I'm here so what can you do to help me with this plan you have?" He told Dock, who had his ice blue glowing eyes, staring at Daniel then Dock stood up and Daniel noticed how taller Dock had gotten.

"We have been waiting for you Daniel. Please do not be scared as we are here to help you to kill off those vampires, we know Drake is here in town and we know it's his blood that is in the drug. We have been looking for him for thousands and thousands of years." Dock announced to Benson.

Daniel had a confused look on his face and replied *"US?"*

Then suddenly Dock came out of the dark and he wasn't human, he was like a werewolf and right behind Dock more of them came out of the dark all of their eyes were all ice blue.

"What the fuck are you guys?" Benson questioned Dock.

"We are Lycans. It's a short word for lycanthrope we are like werewolf's but unlike them we can transform day or night full moon or not we have killed vampires from around the world as well. Once we heard that you are a Dhampir killing the Vampire Gods we had to get involved." Dock confessed as he went back to his human form.

"The Invictus Society knew about me. They let me go. They want to get rid of me and the rest of us." He told Benson.

"So, what is your plan?" asked Benson.

Dock grinned and then he told Daniel the plan. After a few minutes Benson left the hotel room and with a plan for Halloween. He went to his car, and he called up Ally for an update and her location. Once he was done. Where he went to the NYPD building to give her an update. After arriving at the NYPD, he went inside and went to Ally's desk to find her deep paperwork.

"Working late again?" He asked her while holding out doughnuts and coffee for her.

"Just paperwork. Is everything okay now?" she asked as she grabbed the doughnuts and coffee.

"Thank you, but this doesn't make up for what you did to my car. I love that car. When I was growing up, my dad and I struggled. He was a cat burglar. He always talked about having a 1967 Chevrolet Camaro. When I had enough money, I got one. When I showed him pictures, the look on his face was priceless. He is locked up in Rykers doing life. I do see him from time to time. He taught me how to do unlock locks and use a lock pick." She continued. *"When I turned my life around and became a cop, I worked my fucking ass off to get promoted to detective. It is totaled and right now I'm driving a rental until I get another one."* Benson paused for a minute and went into his jacket pocket and grabbed his keys.

"Here! it may not be your dream car, but you can have mine." Benson told Shepard as he handed her his keys to his car. *"Now can you stop bitching please?"* Ally was shocked about what he did for her as a peace offering.

"I don't know what to say. I don't know if I should say thank you or fuck you. But right now, I'll say thanks." She told him he nodded his head as he would take it for now. He sat down to talk to Ally about Drake and what she saw tonight. After what Shepard told Benson he had a worried look on his face.

"I wish he would have shown his face more so you could get a better look. I had nightmares about the same person. I saw his face and what he looked like I have seen him in my nightmares since I was twelve years old." He told Shepard *"I'm sorry I freaked out on you. I didn't mean to freak you out. I may be a bad tough son of a bitch, but once I seen my nightmares come true, I freaked out."* He told her.

After some more coffee and doughnuts, they both were on good terms. They shook it out and they started talking about the case again. Ally asked Daniel about the woman he likes.

"So, that dancer? The one that works with Drake and the rest. What do you see in her?" she asked him.

Daniel paused for a minute and said. *"It started with her eyes. She has the kind of eyes that can look through bullshit. See the good in someone. Twenty percent angel and eighty percent devil. Down to earth. Isn't afraid to get a little blood under her fingernails."* He replied.

"Do you trust her?" She asked him.

"I can sense the good in her. I can tell she has feelings for me. I can sense the grandma in her that I know, and I know she is not afraid to get a little blood under her fingernails." He assured her.

"Let's hope you are right Daniel." Ally assured Benson. Shepard got a call on her phone so, she picked it up. After a few minutes she told Benson some news. *"We may have a witness.*

There was an attempted murder, but he didn't finish, so he took off." She told him.

"Great! Where are we going? it is a male? Let's go! You are driving." He told her.

They both took off to the Bronx to see and interview the witness. Hopefully the victim was okay. After the twenty-minute drive, they showed up while every cop and ambulance were there. They agreed to interview first. Daniel went to question the witness while Ally was headed to try to get to the victim. Once they found where they were going, they headed their own ways. Daniel was going to the apartment building where the witness was. Once he reached the floor, he found a female witness. She was in her late twenties, about five-feet, black hair, chubby, and with tattoos. Once the cops got done interviewing her, Daniel put on his Bogart detective look and approached the witness.

"Hello ma'am. My name is Daniel Benson. Could you tell me what happened?" He asked her.

"Are you a cop? You don't look like a cop." She told him.

"I'm with a different private investigation. I'm working with the NYPD. May I please have your name and what happened here?" asked Benson.

"My name is Mariah Edwards. I was doing my homework in the kitchen with the window cracked up. I then heard a woman scream bloody murder." She explained to Benson.

"Okay, then what happened next?" Benson asked Edwards.

"Are you supposed to be writing this down?" She asked him.

"I have a photographic memory. What happened next please." He questioned her again.

"Then I went and opened up my window. I saw a guy hurting a woman. I yelled at him, and he looked up and saw me. He took off running and that is when I called the cops." Mariah replied.

"Do you remember what he looked like or what he wore?" Benson asked Mariah.

"I don't know. About five-feet-eight. Maybe two twenty, black pants, black boots, wearing a superman shirt, and a camouflage big jacket. He had a superman beanie to cover his hair, and he covered up his face with a mask." Mariah told Daniel.

"Shit that's a damn shame." Benson told Mariah.

"What? That he covered up his face?" She asked him.

"No, that he is a superman fan, gross. Everyone knows Batman is a better superhero. All you have to do to kill off superman is using a damn green rock. Give Superman a kryptonite condom and he will be a limp wimp." He jokingly told Mariah.

She laughed and Benson thanked her for her cooperation, and he left. He went back outside to go see what Ally had on the Victim.

Chapter Thirteen

Ally and Daniel met up once she finished talking to her victim her.

"I talked to the witness. He is male, about five feet eight, two twenty, wearing black pants, with black boots, big camouflage jacket, and wearing a superman shirt with a superman beanie and his face was cover like it was Covid again that is all I know about him." Benson told her.

"Funny, she said the same thing. He spoke to her, he mentioned something about how he needed blood to wake up his love." She explained to him.

Daniel had a confused look on his face. He wondered who else knew about Akasha. He had no time to think about it right now. They needed to find out who the killer was. Then he noticed a few cameras and pointed at them. *"Look, there are cameras on this block. Maybe we can find out who it is. I know it's late now, but let's do it tomorrow and see what we can find out."* Benson told Shepard.

They both agreed and went their own separate ways.

The next day, Daniel was at the Invictus Society building and from what he was told from Ally and the rest of the crew, he was not too happy to hear what happened the last few days.

"What the fuck is wrong with you? How dare you threaten me and my daughter? If you want to kill me, just do it now. Otherwise leave my daughter alone or I will find you and kill you myself boss man. I'm back and once I kill off those fucks, I'm coming for you. So, I hope you leave enough room for my fist, because I'm gonna ram it into your stomach and rip out your goddamn spine." Benson threatened his boss who had no response. *"Figures you don't have a goddamn thing to say. Now if you excuse me, I have a case to solve."* Benson told him and then Daniel left that office. Once he did Gina and April were waiting for him.

"We're sorry. We didn't know what happened to you. We're sorry that we didn't stand up for you and we're sorry that we didn't help you. We are here now," Gina told him.

"I appreciate that ladies, but right now I don't know who to trust. The only thing I can do is try not to get mad at both of you. I'm madder at the boss than you all. Now excuse me. I have to see Thomas about some cameras." He replied to the both of them and then he left that office and headed to see Thomas.

He saw Robert on his way, and he was looking horrible as ever. *"Jesus Christ Robert! You look like shit! Are you sick or what is going on?"* He asked.

"Mind your own fucking business. I know I look like shit! What you and that partner of yours should do is to keep out of my business clear?"

Daniel got mad. He was going to punch him but then he calmed himself down and replied, *"Crystal clear. I'll leave you alone, but if I find out that you are doing some shady shit, I'll kill you too."* He told Robert then he pushed Robert with his shoulder as he walked off to see Thomas.

He then ran into Ally on his way, and they began walking to Thomas' office together.

Once they reached the office of Thomas. They knocked on his door.

"Come in" Thomas instructed them.

"Hey Thomas, this is Ally. She is collaborating with us on this case. There was an attempted murder last night, but someone scared him off. We have a witness and a description. He was wearing a face mask, or I like to call them face panties, but there were also cameras on those side of the blocks."

"Okay cool. Do you have the address?" He asked Benson.

"Yeah, it was on the corner of Murphey and Eagle Ridge It happened around midnight." Benson told him.

"Okay, let me see and check it out. Give me a minute." Added Thomas. After a few minutes of looking back at last night's cameras, he found the footage. *"Here it is. If I can zoom in on his face, we can find out who it is, but the video is so blurry. Luckily for us, I can make this tape clear. Bad news is it will be a few days to do it."* He told them.

"Do it and get back to us when you scrub it. And we can get a clear face." Daniel told Thomas.

He nodded his head yes and they both left the office.

"What now?" asked Ally.

"Just wait. There is nothing else to do. I'm going to go see Leah. Let's hope she doesn't spit at me," replied Daniel.

"I guess I can go see the doctor. She has been waiting to see me for some bloodwork and some DNA test. I have no idea why, but I guess I have too so, I will see you later." Shepard said.

They both went their own ways. Benson was headed to his daughter's room to see what she was doing now. Once Daniel arrived at Leah's room, she was still in a coma, but her fingers were moving here and there.

"Hey babe, it's me, your dad. I know you can hear me. I know you spit at me, but I need you to wake up now. This nightmare is almost over. I need you to wake up so we can go home. I want us to go home." He told Leah. Then she grabbed her hand, and she began to hold Daniel's fingers tight.

"Yes! That's it honey. Please wake up. Hold my fingers again." He told her. She did the same thing. *"Can you wake up now? Can you wake up for daddy?"* He begged her. He got closer to her face to give her a kiss on the forehead, and she spat at him again.

Benson let go of her hand to wipe off his face. Now, being frustrated, he wanted to shake Leah to wake her up, but instead he just stood up to leave. Before he left, he turned around to look at his daughter and announced, *"Wake up for your mother and me. I will kill off that big bitch."* He replied he then left her room, leaving him in the hallways alone. He wanted to cry but he couldn't. That is why he hates his curse. He can't show any emotion. He just wanted to shed a tear. Just for the half human part, but the other half won't let him. Daniel left the hallway and was going to go see Ally and the doctor. After a few minutes he was at the doctor's office who was just finishing up with Ally.

"Ah perfect timing. It's that time again." The doctor noticed him coming in.

"Fine! Whatever! Let's just get this over with." Benson sounded frustrated. After getting some blood and more DNA samples from him, he was all done. Daniel had a call coming in on his phone and he recognized the number.

"I'm glad you called Dock. I think I have a plan to stop these murders. I may need your help." He told him.

"Murders? What murders? You haven't told us about any murders?" He asked Benson.

"Yeah, about that. I had a lot going on but listen, can you meet me in New Jersey? I know this diner there. I'm hungry and need some pie." He asked Dock. They both agreed to meet in Jersey.

Daniel took a cab to go to his storage unit. He paid the cabbie then used his key to unlock the gate. He then walked to his unit. Once he reached it, he used the key again to unlock his storage. He took off the car cover and underneath the car cover was a brand-new Harley Davidson motorcycle. Once he started it up it purred like a kitten. Benson was then off to the diner to meet up with Dock to discuss a plan. After an hour's drive, Daniel made it to the diner. He looked inside and saw no sign of Dock, thinking he was running late. So, he sat outside of the diner and waited for him. After about another hour Dock showed up and once, he found Benson outside and they both went inside and sat down across from one another, and they started to talk.

"So, what about these murders? Why didn't you tell us about them?" Dock asked him.

"We don't know if he is involved or not. The last few weeks, someone has been killing prostitutes and women. Draining their blood. They don't change to vampires." Benson explained.

"Hmm that does sound strange. Well, what do you want us to help you out with?" Asked Dock. Danni came up to their table waiting on their order.

"Oh my god Daniel! It's been forever since we've seen you. Is everything okay?" She asked Benson.

"Yes, everything is fine. Just went M.I.A. for a bit. Anyway, you know what I want and how I like it." He told Danni as she wrote up his order.

"And you stranger?" She asked Dock.

"Just a burger, medium well, and fries." Dock told her. She got both of their orders then Danni took off in the back to make the food.

"So, what is your plan?" Asked Dock.

"Maybe we can lure this motherfucker out and we can capture him and see what he knows. He maybe knows Akasha. We know we have some tech working on the camera outside and two witnesses. This fucker covered up his face, but he likes superman. Those are only the clues we have on him." Benson said.

Danni returned with their food. After taking a few bites Dock had a plan. *"We can use one of our own to be a prostitute and hopefully that can work and see if we can stop it. I shall let you know when and where in twenty-four hours."* Dock told Benson.

After they had dinner, Daniel paid for the meals. They went their own ways. Benson leaned on his bike thinking about what he could do now. But there was nothing he could do. Just try to get some sleep and wait for the call from Dock. So, he got on his bike and started heading home to his loft. After the long drive home. He just wanted to relax. When he reached his floor, he noticed his door was cracked open. Daniel went into the back of his pants to get out his gun and he cocked it. He kicked open the rest of his door.

"FREEZE MOTHERFUCKER!" yelled Benson while pointing his gun at the unknown person. Once that person

heard Daniel's voice, the person turned around, and it was Martha.

"It's been a long-time honey bunny." She told him. She was in a roller walker and on an oxygen tank.

"Oh my god! I almost shot you! What are you doing here? Yes, it has been a long time since we saw each other." Benson was in shock to see it was Martha.

He put his gun away. Amaya showed up out of the kitchen holding two cups of coffee in each hand.

"Hope you don't mind us coming in, but my grandma wanted to talk to you. We went and got ourselves some drinks." Stated Amaya as she was handing one to Martha.

"This is a nice surprise, but for real, what are you doing here Martha?" He asked.

"Well, I may be old, but I can still sense something in you. I have one of those feelings, so I asked Amaya to pick me up and find out where you lived. I can help you. Please sit down." She told him.

Benson did what she asked and grabbed a chair from the kitchen and sat in front of Martha. She was doing something with her hands and speaking tongue. She placed her hands on Daniel's head, and she began the vision. After a few minutes Martha came back, and she freaked out. Almost having a heart attack with what she saw in Benson's vision.

"What happened Martha? Did something happen?" He asked Martha frantically then she went to Amaya, and she whispered something in her ear.

"Ah shit, here we go again. This is 1935 all over again, but I'm not in New Orleans. I'm here in New York." Benson told Martha and Amaya. After Martha got done whispering

something into Amaya's ear, she went and looked at Benson and spoke.

"My grandmother wants to go inside your head again. She wants to double check on what will happen next. She wants to see if anything will happen, and she wants to see into your future again." Amaya told Daniel.

After a few minutes. Benson agreed to let Martha see into his mind and his future and see if it would come true.

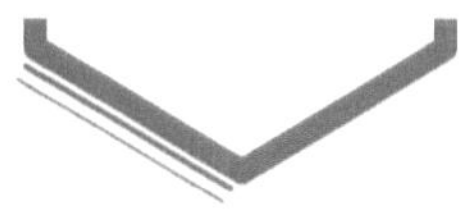

Chapter Fourteen

Daniel sat down across from Martha. She grabbed his hands and started to rub them and then her hands went towards his face the side of his temples.

"Okay, I want you to close your eyes, clear your head, and open your mind. Take deep breaths." She told him.

He did what she asked. He began to take deep breaths in and out. Then he cleared his head of everything and opened his mind. She began to do some tongue speaking chatting then her and Daniel both passed out. They were in a dark place. It had little light showing but not much. This place was so quiet, you could hear a needle drop.

"Wh… where are we?" He asked Martha, confused.

"Inside of your mind. We are here to see what is going to happen in the next few days so we can try to prevent it." She explained to him.

"You think we can stop it? If we find out everything, ahead of time?" He asked.

"It has to work." She noted under her breath.

Just then, more light came in from the darkness and then they could see what was going on in Daniel's mind. It looked like people were fighting. They could both see Amaya and Ally fighting off the minions. While Benson was fighting with a person, they didn't recognize his face because it was blurry.

"How come we can't see this person's face?" He asked Martha.

"I don't know. This is a first for me. This must be the person you fear? Maybe you are scared to see their face." She told him.

Just then, they both saw a knife going through Leah's heart. Then Amaya was dead. Then Ally. Everyone Benson ever encountered was now dead. Even Dock, the last thing they saw was the unknown person picking up Daniel and ripping out his heart to make sure he was dead. Then they both woke up in a cold sweat.

"What the fuck was that, Martha?" He asked Martha.

She grabbed her mask to get some oxygen. *"I don't know, but there is no stopping it. You can't change it."* Replied Martha as she was holding her mask to talk to Daniel so he could hear her.

"Bullshit Martha! You're just old and senile. You are not Doctor Strange. I can and will prevent this from happening. I will change this shit whether you like it or not Martha." He told her.

Then he got up and he went out of his balcony to get some fresh air. Amaya stepped outside to talk to Benson.

"Hey! What happened in there with you two?" She asked.

"We saw everyone die. She was convinced that it couldn't be stopped. Everyone that has been involved with me dies. My heart gets ripped out of my chest by the unknown person." He tells Amaya.

"Maybe we can change that. Did she give you a date and month?" She asked.

"No, I stormed out of there before she could finish. I don't give a damn what she says. I will stop it! I will change it! If that means

I'm the only one who dies and everyone lives, then so be it." He told her as he paced back and forth.

"Fuck! I wish I had a cigar to calm my nerves." Amaya went in front of him to get him to stop pacing.

"Listen, I know you don't want to hear this, but we will work on this, okay? Just let me talk to her but right now. This has been killing me, but here it goes; the people you work with they are not good people. After you are done with your mission, they will kill you and your daughter; if you don't believe me, we have a mole in the Invictus Society. They have been sending me information on them, and on you, and whoever is working for them; or used to worked for them." She told Daniel.

"What the fuck! How can I trust you now? How do I know if you are lying to me?" He asked her angrily.

"I know why your sister really retired. She never told you the truth about what happened." She told Benson.

As the sun began to slowly rise, Benson watched it. He did a big sigh, turned around faced Amaya and he spoke.

"If I find out you are just bullshitting me, I won't hesitate to tell those two fuckers that you are a double agent. Clear?" She nodded her head to the yes motion, *"Good. Now I'm going to get some sleep. I'll call you later. Where do I need to go to find the files on everything?"* Benson asked.

"Under the building of the Invictus Society. The door has a passcode, and the code is 667. The neighbor of the beast." She told him.

After that, Martha and Amaya left Benson's loft so he could get some sleep. It was nighttime when Daniel woke up from his slumber. The first thing he did was to call Dock to see what the plan was to catch this murderer. After a few rings he answered his phone.

"Hello Benson, are you ready to hear the plan?" He asked.

"Yes, tell me what your plan is Dock?" Answered Benson.

"Our plan is that we have one of our own people pretend to be a prostitute. We will all be close so we can find out who this person is. Also, how he knows the queen vampire." Replied Dock.

"I like your plan, Dock. Where are we going to set everything up at?" Benson asked.

"Between 13th and 14th street. We will be hiding behind some big trash bins. We will blend with the people while you and your partner go inside the empty abandoned diner across the way." He explained to Daniel.

"Just give me a time and we will be there." Replied Daniel.

Then he hung up the phone and texted Ally to meet him at the abandoned diner at eleven thirty. She texted with the thumb emoji. He checked his wall clock, and it was almost eleven, so he packed up some guns and some daggers. When he was done, he took off at ten after eleven to head to the diner. By the time he got there it was eleven twenty-five and Ally was already inside the diner waiting for Daniel. He opened the diner doors and was ready for this stakeout.

"How's the car going for you?" He asked her.

"It is fine, thank you again. What are we doing here?" She asked him.

"We are going to find out who the fucker is. He confessed he knew the queen mother. So, we going to find out who he is and what exactly does he know." Benson told Ally.

"So, who is undercover? Do I know her?" She asked.

"No, but here is a picture of what she looks like. So, she is an undercover agent pretending to be a hooker, we are just looking for someone who sticks out." He told her. Daniel heard Dock on his walkie talkie.

"We are in position." He told everyone. "Nobody has come to her yet. She is wired, so once we hear something about who knows who Akasha is. And if they would like to meet her." Dock told Benson on his walkie talkie. After a few hours and no hits, they decided to call it a night. Someone came up to the undercover Lycan asking if they would like to have a threesome with him and his love named Akasha.

"I heard what he said. Get ready guys." Benson told everyone.

"How the hell did you know that? what he said?" Ally Daniel.

"Super hearing I told you before do you remember at the office? Everyone gets ready on my mark!" He told Dock and Ally.

"NOW!" He said.

Then everyone came out of their hiding spots to capture the guy. Daniel and Ally were the first ones to reach him and put him in cuffs. Once Ally stood him up on his feet, Benson removed the guy's hood and mask and was confused. The killer was a homeless man. He searched the guy's pockets front, back, everywhere. No machine, no needles, nothing.

"Let's see what he knows Ally because this is weird." He told her. Ally took the guy to her car and headed to the station while Benson stayed behind. Dock and the rest came up to Daniel and Dock replied.

"Are you okay? Was that our guy?"

"No, that was not our guy. The real killer must of knew or he is hiding. I'm going to go to the station to find out what this homeless dude knows." He told Dock.

Dock just nodded. As they left, Daniel stayed behind for a bit thinking who could have set up this poor homeless man. Daniel was about to leave when he heard a deep cover voice from the dark and it confessed, *"You will never find me. Once my love Akasha is back to herself, we will rule the world together. She told me to do this, and I know every move you make, Daniel. You and that whore detective partner of yours."*

Benson took out his gun just in case the person wanted to come out. Daniel replied to the voice, *"You know, if you were a real man, you would come out of the dark and show yourself. I guess you and Akasha both have one thing in common. That one thing is that both of you are one big giant pussy. Come on out! I promise I won't miss it. They used to call me quick draw Benson because I was fast and first on the trigger."*

The voice never replied. Benson then holstered his weapon and got on his bike and headed towards the station. It began getting foggy. After arriving at the police station Daniel went and started looking for Ally, to see if they could interview the homeless guy together. After asking one of the cops to see where the interrogation room was, Benson headed over there to see Ally. After he found the room Shepard was heading to, Daniel stopped her.

"Ally! Wait a minute. Let's interview this guy together." He told her.

"Why? So, you can put the chair on his neck like last time when I leave?" she asked sarcastically.

"No, I'm being serious. This is not the killer. I mean look at him. He's old and sick and looks like shit." He told her.

"Let us do it. Let's both be good cops. Well good cop and one ex good cop." He told her. After doing some thinking Ally finally agreed to do the interrogation together. They both walked in, and the homeless guy was sleeping. His head was on the wooden table with the ceiling light beaming down on the side of his face.

"Wake up old man. We need you to answer some questions for us." Shepard kicked the back of the chair and then old man jumped.

The old man woke up all groggy, rubbing his eyes, wiped he drool off his face.

"First of all. What is your name and who set you up?" asked Benson.

"My name is Jesus Christ, and I set myself up. She was a sinner, so I had to wash her off her sins." The old man told them Both.

"She was not a sinner. She was an undercover agent! So, I'll ask again, who told you to set yourself up?" Benson asked him again. The old man didn't say a word. He just looked up at the ceiling with a dazed look while humming some church music.

"You know what Ally? I think some coffee will do some good for the three of us What do you think old man? Anything else you want?" asked Benson.

"Chewing gum, candy bar, and my disciples you bitch!" The old man told Daniel.

Chapter Fifteen

s soon as Ally left to get some coffee and the homeless man's stuff. Benson and the old man were alone. Benson was walking around the desk; he told the homeless man. *"Well pops, I guess it's just you, me, your balls, and this drawer."*

Then Benson opened the drawer and slammed it fast. The homeless man's face was scared as he saw Benson's eyes change color and a grin too, showing his fangs. Meanwhile in the hallway Ally was waiting for the coffee to get done. She heard some screams coming from the room and the desk drawer being slammed. The police station was almost empty so, a few police officers stopped to see what was happing. After hearing the screams. Shepard just grinned as well, finally earning Benson's respect. A few minutes later Ally comes in with cups of coffee and the candy bar and gum for the old man. The old man was singing like Taylor Swift saying how it happened and who it was.

"We need a name? Did he say his name?" Shepard asked the old man.

The old man gave Ally the finger and spat at her. *"Sit and spin on this baby or I can give you the real thing."*

"Say Ally wouldn't a couple of doughnuts go great with this coffee right now?" asked Benson as he opened the drawer again.

The old man had a shocked looked on his face as both Daniel and Ally grinned.

October 26[th.] Five days till Halloween.

"So, what we know is that the killer has the same M.O. Killing prostitutes and women. Leaving them dry with no blood he covers up his face wearing superman gear and goes by the name of Kent. He's white and walks like he shits his pants. The Bronx P.D. has some cases as well. They found a few dead people that had holes in their necks, but their blood was still in them. Here is the kicker, the dead bodies come back to life and attacked people and then the same thing all over again." Captain Benjamin told the whole police squad.

Shepard stood in the background. *"If you have any questions, ask Shepard. She has more information. That is, it for today. Watch your backs everyone."* Reported Benjamin as the whole squad was leaving.

"Are you okay? Looks like you haven't slept in a few days?" William asked Ally.

"Well, I'm on the zombie squad. I work nights so yeah, I'm tired." She answered.

"Go home and get some sleep. In fact, take a few days off. If we have anything, I'll let you know. Go home! That's an order." Stated the Captain. When the captain left Ally got out her phone to check the time. It was eight thirty in the morning. She wanted to go home but she needed to go to Rykers to see her dad.

Meanwhile back at the Invictus Society, Daniel had the chance to go down to the building to see what the hell Amaya was talking about. He wanted to know if she was telling the truth about them or not. He took the elevator downstairs and hoped no one was there guarding the doors.

When he heard the ding, the doors opened to reveal a long hallway. The only light Benson could see was the door. He did a super run towards the door. When he got to the padlock, he hit the numbers 667, and it buzzed. He turned the handle, and the door was unlocked. Benson went inside. And was shocked. The Invictus had tons upon tons of files on everything and everyone.

"Well, where do I start?" he asked himself. He decided to start on the society. Where they came from and how they became the Society. Benson started to walk to find the files on the Society. He finally found the file and it was a thick one. He opened it to start reading it.

"The purpose of the Invictus. It was not to defeat empire, but to rule the world for the greater good. We started up in 1667 with our founders. The founders collaborated with the free masons till the free masons wanted to kill the founders. When the founders found out, they ran to the ship heading to the other side of the world. Once the founders decided on where to stay, which was New York, they wanted to rule the world for themselves. When they got more people to recruit, they could kill off people in this world. Over the years the Invictus made deals with the Vatican and with the new world order. Years later The Invictus Society heard something back in the 1900s about zombies being brought back to life in New Mexico. Once they saw and heard about it from a former outlaw by the name of Macayla "Mac" or "Quick gun" McKenzie we had to recruit her to do our dirty work."

"Macayla? Oh my God! I remember her. I remember her and her little girl when Val and I went to see our uncle Peter. It had been a few years since our dad was killed. I remember that entire day. Man, I never knew she was killing zombies. She told us Garrett wanted to do something and she will get pardoned." He replied out loud to himself. He then turned the page to find out more.

"Daniel Benson, we have been watching him since we got his sister on bored. When we heard about what was going on with him, we thought we could get him to do our dirty work as well. It worked. When his sister found out what we were going to do to him after his job was complete. She was going to tell him, but we got to her first. We gave her and her husband the sickness and they both passed away quickly."

"These motherfuckers! They killed them both. Now I'm really pissed off." Then Daniel went to look for his file. He searched until he found it and opened it not expecting what it would say.

"Daniel Benson, Dhampir Vampire. Once he kills off the Gods of Vampires, we must kill him. We have found no weakness of how to kill him till now. Once we kill him, we shall use his daughter to do more killings for us. We killed off his wife Rebecca. We gave her the cancer and it was worth it. Once Drake's deal is done with us, the world will be a better place. First to kill Benson, we need to lure him out. We have discovered a Divine Weapon to kill him and the rest of the Dhampirs. It is called the Staff of Enlightenment. In order for it to work it needs to be charged in the sun for seven days. Once it is fully charged. It can give the staff bright light from the sun. It shoots out a thousand days' worth of light. It will kill off all Dhampirs the staff is made of cedar wood, while the tip of the staff is made from crusted silver and diamond crystal balls. We shall kill Benson once we find it. Once we do that, we need to go to Los Angeles, California for a man by the name of Angel De La Cruz. We are hearing rumors there that he has special powers, we need him."

After Benson finished reading the files on himself. He was pissed, super pissed. He wanted to kill the boss now, but he has to wait and finish the mission and find out what this Devine Weapon was. He found the files on Dock and the Lycans. He took those and the files on him and everyone else. He left before he got caught. He ran back to the elevator. Once the doors opened back up to the stairs, he looked to see if the coast was clear. It was. He wanted to confront the boss, but he was more worried about his daughter, 'till then he decided to wait.

Daniel was heading to Robert's office to see if there were any updates on the Black Thunder or any other weapons. He knocked on his door but no response. So, he opened his door to see if he was in his office. When he opened Robert's office door there were nothing but weapons, blueprints and for some reason a few posters and action figures of Superman. Thinking it could be a coincidence, he thought nothing of it and just waited for Robert. A few minutes later Herrera showed up in his office wearing sunglasses and a coffee in his hand.

"Ah looks like you had a good time last night." He told Herrera.

"Yeah, I finally got some. I was up all night." He replied.

"Well, you can stop being a bitch now. Listen, I just noticed your superman stuff. Have you been a fan long?" Benson questioned him.

"Yes, for a long time. I can tell you everything about him if you want?" He answered Benson.

"No, it's okay. I want to see if you have any new toys for me or updates?" Replied Benson.

"As a matter of fact, I just got done with the Black Thunder if you want to test it out?" He said.

"Sweet, let's go test it out." Benson told Herrera. They both heading to the testing shooting rage to test out the Black Thunder.

When Daniel forgot he had the files he took from under the building. He was hoping that Robert wouldn't ask him to take off his leather jacket. Once they reached the testing range, they both stopped while Robert took a kneel on the floor and put the bag down. He then unzipped it and took out the Black Thunder. The look on Benson's face was exciting because he had never seen a gun like this before.

"Okay sir, here it is, the Black Thunder. One of my best weapons yet. You put this big sucker on your back like a backpack and you unhook the weapon part like taking the shotgun out over your shoulder. Hang on, let me turn it on for you. When it hums, that means it is working. Do you mind taking off your coat? That's the only way it will work." Herrera told him.

Benson was hesitant about it. He had no choice but to do it. He tried his best to hide the files under his jacket, so Robert wouldn't see them. Once he hid the files under his jacket he went back to Robert, then he started to put the suit on.

Once Robert turned it on, they both waited for it to humm. Once it did, Daniel rubbed his hands together, grinning from ear to ear.

"Okay sir, where is the trigger?" He asked Robert.

"That big red button. Just aim at your target, hit the button, and watch the magic come alive." He added.

He turned around and found wooden boxes and paper targets. Once Benson saw his target, he hit the red button and bolts of lightning started to come out BOOOOMMMMM. Everything that Benson targeted just exploded. After he took his thumb off the button, he told Robert.

"Holy shit! I love this gun goddamn. I could kiss you, Robert! This makes up for all the other weapons you have made." Benson told him as he was taking the weapon off his back.

Robert announced. *"What are you going to do with this weapon now?"*

Chapter Sixteen

"*Hopefully kill off that big bitch and the rest of those dead fucks.*" He told Herrera.

Then suddenly, Robert took off power walking like he was in a hurry.

"*Where are you going Herrera?*" asked Benson.

Robert didn't answer, he just kept walking out of the room.

Daniel was confused about why he left in a hurry. "*What the fuck is his problem?*" Noted Daniel.

He wrapped up his new gun and headed upstairs. He went upstairs to see Robert in his office. He walked into his office, and he was not there. Benson was going to look for him some more until he got a call on his cell. He checked his phone to see who it was, and it was Thomas.

"Thomas, I hope you got some good news for me man." He told Croft.

"As a matter of fact, I do. I found a camera that shows the killer's face. Before he puts on his mask, so call your partner, I'll be in my office." He told Benson.

After he was done talking to Thomas, he called up Ally. After a few rings she answered.

"Hey what's up?" She asked.

"Thomas got the camera up. He has the killer's face on camera. We are waiting for you." He told her.

"I'm on the way now." She replied.

After they both hung up, he went straight to Thomas' office, where Thomas was waiting. They were waiting for Shepard to show up. Daniel stopped April and Gina to give them updates, and he told them to see who it was as well. All three of them were waiting on Ally in Croft's office. when she showed up.

"Oh, wow okay. The whole gang is here," said Croft.

"Yeah. Yeah, cut the shit. Show us who it is," demanded Benson.

"Okay. I fixed the tapes. When I looked at them, they were blurry but now with this recent technology, we can make everything clear. So here it goes. As you can see the killer getting out of the car. I can't see the plate number on it, but he thinks he is smooth trying to look for every camera. He forgot this one hiding in the corner. So, ladies and gentlemen, here is your killer's face clear as a bell." Croft told everyone.

Once the camera tape zoomed in on the face of the killer. After taking off the pixels everyone was shocked, and their mouths dropped. The killer was none other than Robert.

"WHAT THE FUCK!" Daniel exclaimed.

He was so furious his blood red eyes were seen through his sunglasses.

"Where is this motherfucker? I'm going to kill him. I'm going to kill off that bitch. Where did he go? Thomas, can you find him in the building? See if he left yet." He asked Croft.

"Shit, I don't know. Let me see." He told Daniel as he typed away on his keyboard.

After checking every camera inside the building, they found him heading to Akasha.

"Get extra security and tell them to go to Akasha's cell now!" Daniel ordered.

Now on full alert, Benson and Shepard make haste and hustle their way to Akasha's cell. Upon their shock and disbelief when everyone arrived, they saw Robert. But unbeknownst to them, he's decked out in full riot gear, body armor, and enough weapons to his own against a full battalion. Benson takes his gun, aims at Herrera, and speaks. *"ROBERT FREEZE! YOU'RE SURROUNDED! THERE'S NO ESCAPE!"* shouts Benson. At the top of his lungs. Robert, being the savvy tech guy that he is, has a detonator that is synced to the explosives that are strategically placed beneath the cell floor holding up a remote detonation device. Robert shouts back in sheer pain coming from his voice.

"YOU CAN'T DO THIS TO ME! DON'T TAKE AWAY MY LOVE!" Repositioning himself, taking a few steps back, he bellows out. *"I LOVE HER WITH ALL I HAVE!"* Activating his remote sensors the floor lights up. *"IF YOU KILL ME, EVERYONE AND EVERYTHING WITHIN THIS BLOCK GOES UP IN FLAMES AND RUBBLE! I'M HERE FOR AKASHA, THAT'S ALL! SO, ALL OF YOU DO YOURSELFS A FAVOR AND PUT YOUR GUNS DOWN NOW!"*

"Okay, we're listening to you. Just relax and listen to me out, okay? She's in your head, she's using you. You have to come to your senses." Daniel tried to convince him. As he, Shepard, and the entire security team slowly begin to lay their firearms down. *"Come on dude, you're better than this. I can protect you. Just let*

this thing go, come with me and you will be fine, okay. She's not good for you. She's going to destroy you and ultimately kill you once she's done." Benson continued. As he tries to take a step closer to the estranged Robert.

"NO! YOU DON'T UNDERSTAND! SHE'S THE LOVE OF MY LIFE. I FINALLY HAVE A PURPOSE, AND SHE'S GIVEN ME HOPE SINCE MY WIFE LEFT ME AND TOOK MY KIDS. I WANTED TO KILL MYSELF BUT AKASHA GAVE ME A NEW LIFE AND BEGINNING!"

Benson walked closer to Herrera. Robert noticed him and announced, *"DON'T YOU COME ANY CLOSER BENSON! I'LL END IT ALL HERE AND NOW!"* Screamed Robert as he tightened his grip on the remote.

"Okay! Okay! You got it man." Replied Benson as he stopped walking.

He and the others slowly backed away. All attention was focused on Robert's hand and thumb poised to hit the button. Then suddenly Robert showed everyone an evil grin as he hit the button.

(BEEP)

Within seconds the concrete ground began to shake and tremble violently knocking Benson, Shepard, and the rest of the team off their feet. Several explosions go off as they start destroying the floor beneath them.

BOOOOM

BOOM

BOOM

BOOOOM

With smoke and ash and debris rising from under the destruction, the entire area was blanketed with pitch black smog, fire, and heavy dust. Benson, Shepard, and the security team began coughing, choking and unable to breathe as they were sent to confusion. Daniel, taking a major chance, gets to his feet, gets his gun, and starts to charge in Robert's direction only to discover a massive hole in the ground. Robert and Akasha were gone.

"THAT SON OF A BITCH! I'M GOING IN." Daniel yelled to the others.

He jumped down the deep dark hole. When Daniel went down the hole, he saw some light. He landed on his feet like a cat. If a normal person did this, they, would have died.

"Ally, can you hear me!" Asked Benson.

"Yes, should I come down!" She replied.

"No, I need a flashlight and an automatic sub gun." He confessed.

After a few minutes. Ally came back with a gun and flashlight. She tossed them to Daniel.

"Get out of here. See if you can find him on the streets. I found some tracks. I'll follow them to see where they lead." He told her.

Benson locked and loaded up the gun. He turned on the flashlight and followed the tracks Herrera left behind.

"These are some fresh track marks. It looks like Robert used some sort of machine to drag the mega bitch." Benson told himself.

He continued to follow the tracks. He found Robert about a hundred yards away putting Akasha in the bed of his truck. Daniel came out of hiding, pointed the sub machine gun at Robert and spoke.

"Robert, you dumb son of a bitch, it's all over. Let go of the mega bitch!" He demanded Robert.

He ignored Benson's orders as he climbed inside of his truck. Before he could get inside, he grabbed a 12-gauge shotgun, turned around, and started to shoot at Benson. Daniel went behind some big barrels as Herrera kept firing at him then. He ran out of shells and his shotgun clicked. Benson came out from behind the barrels, and he shot at Robert, but he was already inside the truck pulling away. Benson got a few shots back before he started to run at the truck. Then Benson put the sub machine gun over his shoulder as he reached for the truck. He did a big jump on the roof of the truck just to hang on for dear life. Robert tries his best to get Daniel off the truck. He went left and right in the tunnels to get him off while doing almost a hundred miles an hour.

Once Benson saw daylight, he knew they would reach the city, so he held on as Robert did a powerful sideswipe. Benson had to stop him now and quickly. So, Daniel got off the roof and worked his way to the front window of the truck. Once he did that, he still had that sub machine gun, and he pointed it at Robert. He started swerving left and right to shake Benson off the truck. Benson dropped the gun. Benson had no other choice but to break the window with his leg. After a few kicks, the window began to break, and just as Daniel was about to do one more kick to break the window, Robert shot him in the chest with the 12-gauge shotgun knocking him off the truck. Benson fell and rolled off the hood of the truck. All Daniel could do was watch Robert leave with Akasha. Being defeated and bleeding, people ran up to Daniel to see if he was okay. He heard sirens and, in the distance, he could see Ally and the rest of the NYPD show up to see if Benson caught Herrera.

Shepard got out of her car and just ran straight towards Benson to see if he is all right. *"What happened?"* She asked. Benson was getting up from the ground. *"That son of a fucking bitch shot me and left. I almost had his ass and now we lost our only lead!"* Stated Benson as he began to heal from his wound. He was up on his feet already walking.

"Where are you going?" Shepard questioned him.

"Jersey!" He yelled.

"How?" She replied.

"I'll goddamn walk!" He yelled. Benson, started to walk to New Jersey to the diner and to clear his head.

When Daniel was walking to New Jersey, the weather was not kind to him. It went from cold, to freezing rain, then to fog, but he was going to make the walk to the diner. He crossed the bridge from New York to New Jersey. He stopped at the middle of the bridge, and he leaned over it. Thinking about hopping over the bridge and jumping into the icy water. He has tried everything so he might as well jump just to end it. Benson was going to do it when he heard a voice coming from the fog.

"So, you came back to life one more time. You fought through the torments alone and you want to end it now?" Amaya told Benson.

"Why me? Why was I chosen for this? There has to be someone better than me!" He shouted in anger, never believing himself worthy of being a hero.

"No one chose you." She responded softly. *"You chose yourself. You stood when no one else could. Being a hero doesn't always mean you're destined for it or chosen by some higher power.*

Sometimes standing up against the great evil when no one else can, knowing you may very well fall to it is enough to be a hero." She told Benson as their eyes were locked.

"We can do this. We can stop this. Please just take my hand." She told him.

Daniel thought about it, and he decided to take Amaya's hand. Right then and there is something about Amaya. Her aura, her eyes and spirit, that Benson has falling for her. As they got in her car.

"Where are we going?" Benson asked.

"My place in Staten Island. No one knows where this place is at. It will be safe there." She told him as they took the 45-minute drive from the city to Staten Island.

Chapter Seventeen

After the 45-minute drive they arrived at Amaya's place. It was an abandoned amusement park. The theme of the park was based off an old television show. The show was a hit in the late 80s and early 90s, but the ride didn't do good to the public, so it was left abandoned never to be open again.

"Well, at least I get to have fun in here." Benson told Amaya.

"No one knows about this place. Not even my grandma Martha. You are safe here." She told Daniel.

They went inside the building; it was a sad old thing. It was somehow still working. After going through the maze of this park, they finally made it to Amaya's place. Once they went inside, there wasn't much. Just a kitchen, television, one couch and a punching bag in the corner. Benson kept walking, she had no kitchen table, and the bathroom was small. Just a stand in the shower. She went to her bedroom. The bedroom was huge. It has a queen-size bed and two dressers. Once he left, he saw another room, it was full of weapons, blueprints, and books. He was about to leave until he noticed a note with a notebook next to it. He wanted to read it but not with Amaya around. He heard Amaya in the kitchen making noise, so he closed that door behind him and went to see what she was doing.

"Do you need any help?" He asked her.

"No, I'm just going to make some tea." She told him.

As she was making tea, Benson stood behind her admiring her and scoping her out. He wanted to make sure that she was a person he could trust. She went and grabbed two-fold up chairs in the hall closet. She offered Daniel a seat while they waited for the tea to finish. After the tea maker made the whistling sound, she grabbed two cups and poured the tea. She offered one of the teas to Benson. When he got the tea, he was wishing it was a bottle of Jack Daniels or even some blood. *"This will do for now."* He replied.

"So, tell me about the people you work for. Why are you undercover?" Stated Benson

"Like I said, I work for Sacred Fire. We are Native Americans that solve cases involving the Paranormal, the Spirit realm, Demons and of course Vampires and Werewolves." She explained to Daniel.

"Well, you picked a hell of a bad week to investigate the vampires. The Vampire that we had locked up for a long time is gone now. Gone, someone I know, I thought I could trust, broke her out of her jail cell and took off to God knows where." Replied Benson.

"You mean Akasha?" She asked him.

"Yes. Let me guess, Martha told you about her?" He asked.

"Well yeah, she told me. I heard from my informants on the inside as well."

As they both take a sip of their teas.

"I looked at my files of the Invictus Society. You were right and so was Dock. They want to kill me when the mission is completed. They do know a way to kill me off. Something about

Staff of Enlightenment? I just looked at the history and my files and some files on the Lycans. Shit! I forgot the files. Motherfucker! I got to go." Stated Benson.

He slammed his tea then stood up. He began feeling dizzy and sick when he realized he hadn't had any blood in a few days. He was all out of pills, and he didn't bring his blood gun with him. Daniel kept spinning until he finally fainted on the floor.

When Daniel came too, it was early morning. He was on Amaya's bed all healed up, but she was nowhere to be found. He felt like death. He thought it was 24 hours, so he got up and started looking for her, but first he went and checked his cell phone to see what time it was. Once he checked it, it was dead. He went to find a charger to charge it. He found one in the kitchen. He didn't want to charge it all the way, so he went and half-charged it. Then he was curious about that note and notebook, so he went to the room where they were. His eyes were only on that notebook and paper. It could be clues? He went and opened the notebook he flipped through it. It looked like a journal entry. He went to the last entry.

"October 28th, Daniel has been sleeping for the last two days. I have been sleeping next to him on the air mattress. He just sleeps. I caught him rolling his eyes in his sleep. I have to watch him. My grandma Martha was right! He is special. I will do what I must to help him out and get his daughter back. I'm heading back to the club to see what Koi and Rebekah are up to. I just hope Benson is still sleeping when I get back."

Benson was shocked. He was out for two fucking days. He then went to check the note. Maybe it was a clue.

"We have been tracking Angel De La Cruz from Los Angeles. He keeps mentioning some visions. De La Cruz is a LAPD Detective who keeps talking about some legend in Mexico called the Montezuma. We will let Amaya, and the rest of the Sacred Fire know about this case."

"Shit! Not again! I have been out for two days and what the fuck is this about some Montezuma? Good luck De La Cruz. You are going to need it kid." Noted Daniel He still had a shock look on his face. The last time he slept that long was in 1935 at Rebecca's house. He left the room and went to go check his phone. He went to the kitchen to see if his phone was charged. It was at twenty percent. He turned on his phone and he had several missed calls from Shepard and the Invictus Society.

"Fuck, I know the Society knows about the files. Let me see." He knew he was in trouble. He then called them.

After a few rings, they picked up. "BENSON!" as it was the boss on the other end. "Benson you are a piece of work. Do you think we are fucking stupid? Why did you take those files? Who gave you the password?" The boss angrily asked Benson.

"Because I want to know who the fuck I'm working for. I should kill your ass for killing my sister, and my wife. Should I call the free masons? Or the New World Order?" He told the boss.

The boss gave Daniel an evil laugh. "I should kill your daughter. But you know what I'll do one even better if I was you, I would watch your back because now you are a wanted man" the boss told Daniel.

"What the fuck are you talking about?" Benson asked.

"I knew about Robert's little adventure. Let's say that you helped him with those murders." He threatened Benson.

"The cops won't believe you. I'm working with the cops you asshole." He reminded him.

"WE OWN THE COPS AND THE NEWS NETWORK! Whatever we tell them, they go with it. So good luck Benson. You will never see your daughter again, and it will feel good to pull the plug on her coma ass on Halloween!" The boss then hangs up the phone.

Benson, being more pissed, punched a hole through Amaya's brick wall. He had to call Shepard. After a few rings, she answered her phone.

"Daniel! What the fuck is going on? I know you didn't do it, but they have an APB on you and Robert for murder." She told him.

"I know, they found the files that I took on that I was looking at. I'm not in the city. I'm hiding out. I have to get to the city to meet up with you." He told her.

"Are you fucking crazy. They will arrest you on the spot." She warned him.

"I have to get my weapons. We don't have much time left. Do what you can and call me back." He told Shepard. She paused then finally said something. "Fine, but Benson, watch your ass please?" She told him, before hanging up.

Daniel was leaving Amaya's place. He left a note for Amaya to let her know what was going on. When he made his way out of the old amusement park, the weather was getting bad. He had no time to stop. He had to get to his loft to get his weapons and come back to Amaya's hideout. He tried to get a cab, but it was hard as the city was like a ghost town with the storm coming in. He finally found a taxi to take him back to the city. After an easy drive to the city, he got to his loft, left a cabbie a good tip and he was back outside. The weather was still shitty. The wind was so powerful that it was blowing trash bins, mailboxes and trash. Benson even saw a big tree fall on the street. He had to stop this nightmare. He was having a hell of a time walking to the door to his loft. He reached the door and opened it up and had to slam it to close. He was safe inside. Once he reached his loft, he noticed that his door was open a bit. He figured someone had broken in. Daniel was unarmed so he couldn't defend himself. He opened the door slowly. Once he entered, it was not ransacked. He heard a noise coming from the kitchen. Benson was like a cat. He walked quietly to the kitchen door, and he heard voices coming from the other side. He opened the door prepared to fight. He was shocked to see who it was. It was April, Gina, Dr. Lovato, and her nurse Carla.

"What the hell are you guys doing here?" He asked them.

"We're here to help you," replied April.

"Why should I trust you all? What if you are trying to kill me?" He asked them.

"Look, I know what is going on. You didn't do it. We are on your side. Trust us Daniel. Please." Explained Gina.

Just then, Andrea was getting something out of her purse. She pulled out more blood pills.

"Looks like you can use these. You are looking pale and it's your favorite blood type." She handed him the pills.

Benson was hesitant to take them. But he did anyway, he just took half of the bottle and started to feel better after that. He didn't look pale anymore.

"How the hell did you get inside my loft?" Benson questioned them.

"I did." Replied Shepard. Daniel turned around to see who was behind him. It was Ally.

"So, what's the plan?" asked Ally.

"I don't know yet. I'm still thinking this over, but if I do trust you all, then my only plan for now is to watch out for my daughter. Once midnight hits on October 31st that fucker is going to kill my daughter. I want you to try to stop him and the rest of them." Benson told them.

They all nodded and agreed. They started to leave when Gina and April stopped, turned around, and looked at Benson. April was getting something out of her Pocket. *"Here take this. Just push the button and that button will do the rest."* Explained Gina.

"What's this for?" He asked them.

"Call it a big, huge backup." April replied before they continued to leave.

Shepard and Benson were alone. *"What do you want me to do on my end?"* asked Shepard.

"Figure out where that backstabbing bitch ass punk is at. I know there is an ABP on him and me. Try to convince your boss I didn't do it." He told her.

She nodded her head as she was leaving.

Daniel just stood in the middle of his loft apartment. Thinking how he could do this again. Once his head and mind were clear, he went to his fireplace. There was a big picture, and the picture was a safe with number codes on it. Once he put the code in, the fireplace suddenly started to move. It revealed weapons galore. He went and got a big black duffle bag. Stocked and loaded up on every weapon he had that killed vampires. Then he got his custom-made Katana sword that was on the sword mantel. This sword had all the Gods of Vampires names on it. There are only two names left on the sword. *"Damn shame I didn't use this on Klaus. Oh well, the other two will have the same fate."* He confessed.

He could feel the power of the sword as he held it for a few more minutes. Daniel then put the sword behind his back.

Once he was done loading up, he looked at his family picture. He took it out of the picture frame and took it with him. Then he went to his bedroom closet. He was looking at his old trench coat and his dad's lucky fedora hat. Also, the gold dagger. He dropped the bag. Daniel put on his trench coat, his dad's hat, he picked up the dagger along with the tommy gun. They still made bullets to this day. He picked up his duffle bag, and he stood for a quick moment. Closed his eyes and thought about everything that was going on. Once he opened his eyes, they changed to glowing red, and his fangs came out. He was now pissed off. The blood pills worked. He told himself, *"Send a maniac to catch some maniacs."*

He then opened his door and realized he had company.

Chapter Eighteen

"*S orry I don't do threesomes.*" Daniel joked sarcastically.

Two minion vampires were waiting for him at his door. With one big punch, he knocked one vampire's head off. The other one was scared and was going to run but Benson grabbed the other one by its neck. Then lifted the minion vampire in the air and punched its heart out. The bodies started to turn into dust. Daniel went to his bag and got out a few guns and a custom made 12 gage shotgun. He made his way outside. Once he opened the door, the horror began. The weather had stopped. Benson saw people running for their lives, as thousands of minion vampires were killing and eating innocent people. Daniel could only do so much to help. He was shooting minions left and right. He had to get back to Amaya to see if she was alright. Benson was leaving, he had no choice but to leave people behind. He was headed to Staten Island upset and disgusted at himself because he couldn't do anything. He was hoping Ally and everyone else was safe and hoping they were armed. He was driving and hauling ass. He killed a few vampires along the way, hitting them with a random car he found on the side of the road.

Once he reached Staten Island, he realized it hadn't hit there yet. It won't be long. Once he reached the bridge, the weather was cold and raining again. He reached her hideout; he got out of the car leaving his coat and hat and the tommy gun behind. Along with the gold dagger and his sword. He took out his gun and left the rest of his guns in the car. He was headed to the building. He stopped when he saw headlights in the distance. He saw a figure in the car while blocking the headlights with his hand. The figure came out of the car, and it was Amaya. From the look on her face, she was shocked and bloody. She just went right in without saying anything to Daniel. He followed her, trying to say something to her, she didn't say anything. Then Benson finally caught up to her and spoke.

"Wait! Wait just a minute! Talk to me!" He grabbed her arm.

"What are you so scared of? What do you want?" She asked him.

The things I want by Daniel Benson; a cigar. A shot of Jack. For the sun to shine. I want to sleep to forget. To change the past. I want my wife and baby girl back. Unlimited ammo and for this nightmare to end. But right now, more than anything, I wanted her.

He grabbed Amaya and pulled her towards him. He kissed her hard and passionately. She didn't resist. He leaned her against the wall, and he placed her arms up above her head. He started to kiss her stomach, and she began to moan while interlocking her fingers in his hair. She took off her leather jacket and Benson lifted her bloody shirt, exposing her breast. When he got done kissing her stomach, he lifted her up by her ass and they started kissing more. They made their way to the bedroom to have sex.

The last few nights they were still in bed resting up. Benson got up first and he sat up on the edge of the bed feeling guilty about what had happened. Amaya was right behind him waking up. She kissed his neck to let him know she was up. She could sense what was going on. She covered up and started talking to him.

"What's wrong? Is everything okay?" She asked him.

"Yeah, just feeling guilty about the people. I wanted to save them all, but there were too many vampires." He told her.

"We will beat them. We will kill Koi and Rebekah, and we will get your daughter back." She told him as she got up from the bed still naked.

She headed to the bathroom to get dressed. Benson decided he should get dressed too. After he was done, he went to his coat pocket to get out the picture of him, Rebecca, and Leah. He grinned a bit, then he heard a noise. He grabbed his gun and went to see what the noise was and where it was coming from. He looked out the window and he saw vampires coming inside the building. He also saw Koi and Rebekah standing outside of the building giving orders.

"SHIT AMAYA. HURRY UP THEY ARE COMING!" He yelled at her.

She ran out of the bathroom already armed and ready. She had weapons hiding in the bathroom.

"Where did you hide those toys?" He asked her.

"Oh, I have my ways." She grinned.

They got closer to each other and kissed before going separate ways. She went left and he went right.

Daniel was on a roll killing more minions as they came in. He made his way down the stairs of the building, blasting every minion that came close to him. The area was full of ashes. Once he made it down the stairs, he started looking for Amaya. He wanted to make sure she made it out of there as well. Benson forgot the maze part of this park but luckily for him he knows away around it. Around every corner there were minions, he went to shoot more but he ran out of bullets. One of them was headed straight for him. He heard shots coming from above him. He looked up and seen Amaya. She was shooting them with her sniper rifle. She must have gotten that from another hiding spot. Once she killed other surrounding minions, she looked back down at Benson, and they smiled at each other. Then they were off running again. When Benson finally made it to the front door, he waited on Amaya so they could walk out together. Then suddenly he heard a voice coming from outside.

"DHAMPIR! COME OUT HERE NOW! WE HAVE SOMEONE FOR YOU!" It was Koi's voice.

Daniel went outside, and it was Koi, Rebecka, and more minion vampires. They even had the place surrounded by cops that they had turned into vampires. Thunder and lightning battled in the sky as the rain fell even harder than before. The minions were holding Amaya hostage. She struggled to break free but stopped when a knife was placed to her throat.

Koi and Rebecka were holding umbrellas and wearing gloves to protect themselves from the rain. They stood in front of a black limousine.

"Santanico! How could you do this to me? How did you fuck this good looking Dhampir before me?" Rebecka asked Amaya.

Benson walked slowly towards them trying to think of a plan to save Amaya. There were so many of them.

"That's far enough Dhampir. So, tell me, how does it feel to finally be the one on the short end of the stick?" asked Koi.

Benson held his hands up in the air and told Koi and Rebecka. *"You know what? You all won. You will rule the world, but you should be thanking me. I let your queen mother Akasha escape. With a guy named Robert, who I thought was my friend. So, if you want her, you just have to go get her. So, I can kill each one of you and let this nightmare end."* He confessed.

Daniel kept his hands in the air as car lights beamed at him. The driver of the limo honked its horn at both Koi and Rebekah. Rebekah ordered one of the minions to hold Amaya while the rest of them kept their eyes on Benson. He and Amaya locked eyes. They both thought this would be the last time they ever saw each other again. Daniel's skin was burning from the rain. He had to think of something fast. He knew if he moved a muscle, he would be dead and there was no way he could try to save Amaya then.

They both heard yelling and shouting coming from the limo and from Koi and Rebekah. After a few minutes of going back and forth, they both came back. Rebekah held Amaya while Koi started talking.

"Looks like the doctor wants you dead. Since Queen Akasha has escaped, he can finally be reunited with her. Any last words from you? You half human half vampire disease!" Koi asked Daniel.

"Yeah, I do. Go fuck yourself!" Benson told Koi.

With one final move with his hands, two guns came out of his jacket. He started shooting at whatever was in his way. When he ran out of bullets, he went back inside the building. Koi now really pissed off ordered the police officers to start shooting at the building. They kept shooting till they hit the big propane tank that goes into the building. Once they hit that, the building went up in big, huge flames, blowing everything up including Daniel. Everyone was happy and cheering. Amaya was shocked, she put her hands over her mouth and began to cry. Then Rebekah grabbed her by the hair and started to drag her to the car. Amaya was not going to fight. There were more minions than her. Once they got into the limo, they headed to the club. The minions were right behind them.

October 30th. Twenty-four hours before Halloween. Early morning as the building was starting to settle down, someone was moving the metal walls and bricks looking for Daniel. He was still alive, but in and out of consciousness when the brick and metal was out of his face, he could see someone. His vision was too blurry to see but they dragged him by his leg just to get him out of there. The rain had stopped, but it was just sprinkling. It hit his face, then he was out again. When he came too, he was somehow bandaged up and lying on a bed. He tried to get out of bed, but he was still healing. He looked at his right arm and it was still healing from the third-degree burns. He could see his bone and burned skin as he took one of his bandages off. He struggled to walk. He wanted to get out of the room. He had to lean on the wall to get going. Once he finally reached the door, he opened it, and he fell right back down. Someone picked him up. It was Dock.

"How did you find me?" asked Benson as he was still struggling to get up.

"We followed those two to where you were at. We watched and waited for the time to attack but they blew up the building. I had

my people follow them while I stayed and waited for the building fire to go out." Dock replied to Benson.

"You took your Lycan ass time getting to me." He replied.

"I know. You were going to be fine. You will heal up in a few hours." Dock told him.

Call the NYPD and ask for Detective Ally Shepard. Let her know what happened. If you can't reach her, try her cell." Benson told Dock. Then Benson passed back out from the pain. A few hours later Benson came too. The burn marks and broken bones healed up on their own. Dock was in front of him, along with Ally. She was shocked at how fast he healed.

"When I first saw you...you had bandages all over you. Just the right side of your face was good. But wow, it takes what? A normal person takes years to heal from those kinds of burns. Are you feeling better now?" She asked him.

He stood up and checked his body and it healed fast and good and then he assured Shepard. *"Yeah, I'm good. What happened?"* He asked.

"New York is filled with those ugly fucks. The cops I worked with are either dead or turned. Or they left town. Only a few are left. Even the captain decided to stay to fight, and he told me to give this to you." Ally handed something to Benson.

Once Daniel grabbed it from Ally's hand, he opened his hand, and it was none other than a NYPD badge.

"I know this is not the wild west or the south. But he said that you are now deputized. I don't know what he meant by that." Explained Ally.

"This means I work for you all. Just as a volunteer. It's been a long time since I wore one of these. 1930, last time I checked." Replied Daniel.

"Okay so what's the plan?" Dock asked.

"The plan is this, first we load up. Ally and I will get every weapon there is and then we send those dead demon fucks back to hell. Dock does your people still know were Koi and Rebekah are at?" Benson asked Dock.

"Yes, they are at the club. It's guarded heavily. My people can't go in without being shot down. Even being human, they are shot down because it's a private party tonight." He told him.

"Well shit! We have two ways to enter. One, we go in with guns blasting or two, we go in there with a vehicle and smash the door and start blasting." Daniel suggested.

After thinking about it for a minute, they all agreed to do number two.

"What time is it by the way?" Benson asked.

"Nine forty-five. Why?" asked Shepard.

"My daughter's life could be in danger at midnight on Halloween." He told Shepard.

Just then, Dock came back and had Benson's duffle bag with his weapons, his coat, and hat.

"Well, good thing you saved these in the car. You left these in your car, even your phone and this?" Dock was holding the button.

Benson grinned at him and took the button from Dock. *"Well, I guess this is now or never."*

After a few pushes nothing happened. Then, suddenly, the three of them heard noises coming from outside. Benson and Shepard loaded up on guns while Dock went to his form, ready to fight. The door was kicked in so hard it flew across the room and hit the wall.

A tall figure with red eyes was standing outside of the door staring at them until he finally spoke up. *"Who pushed the button?"* asked the figure in a deep scary voice.

"I did. I guess you're the backup? Just one person?" Benson asked the creature.

"I'm not one person. There are many more like us." The figure told Benson.

"Us?" Benson tilted his head in confusion as he lowered his gun.

the figure showed himself. *"Yes, us, the Dhampirs. We have been hiding and waiting for someone to push that button so we can fight with the rest of the vampires."* Announced the Dhampir.

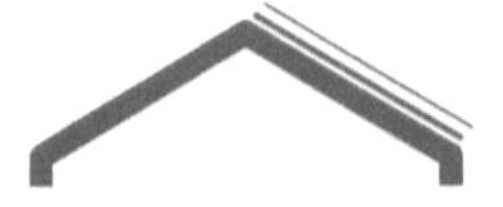

Chapter Nineteen

Just then, Benson and Shepard put their guns away and started walking outside. When the Dhampir moved out of the way, Benson and Shepard saw millions of Dhampirs. One of the Dhampirs reached his hand out for a shake.

"Arnold of the year 1400s." He replied to Benson.

"Daniel Benson, 1935." They both shook hands, then he shook Shepard's hand.

"Why were you all hiding? Why didn't you help when I needed you?" He asked Arnold.

"We were hiding and waiting for someone to push the trigger. This place called the Invic..."

Benson stopped him right there. *"The Invictus Society lied to you. They never needed help. They just wanted to rule the world like these fucking vampires. Once I am done killing them all, they are going to kill me and my daughter."* He told Arnold.

"I'm sorry to hear about that. But we are here now, and we are here to fight alongside you and your human partner here." He assured Benson.

"Well, I hope you get along with Lycans, because it's fucking war now. Arnold, I hope you and the rest of the Dhampirs are ready and armed. I hope you learned how to shoot while you were hiding?" Benson told him.

"We did and we are ready good sir?" He replied to him.

"New plan then. Half of the Dhampirs fight in the street to kill off the vampires and try to save as many people as possible, while the others fight with us. Dock, call your people and tell them we got back up! Lots of back up." He told Dock.

As they were getting ready for the new plan. Benson checked his phone, and he noticed he received a call from a number he didn't know. He called it back and after a few rings someone answered. It was a male on the other line.

"Hi, is this Daniel Benson?" The male voice asked.

"Yes, it is. May I ask who is calling?" Benson replied.

"Yeah, hi this is Bruce Watchman. I am one of Martha's great grandkids. I'm just letting you know that she passed away in her sleep late last night. In one of her notes, it noted to call you if something happened to her. We tried calling Amaya, but we can't get ahold of her," Bruce said.

"I'll make sure she gets the message. I know she is at work right now, but when I see her, I will let her know. Thank you. Goodbye." He told Bruce.

Once he got off the phone with Bruce. Daniel wanted to cry but he couldn't. All he could do was think about how he and Martha had that great night in New Orleans when they slept together. She saved him and knew about the Invictus Society. She stayed in New York just to keep watch over Daniel.

When everyone was ready to go to battle, Benson, Shepard, and Dock all went in one car while the army of Dhampirs followed Daniel's lead. Dock was driving. Ally was in the passenger seat while Benson was in the back putting bullets in the clips of his guns and double checking them. He then put his trench coat on and his dad's lucky fedora hat. When they left it was around ten so they should get to the city on time.

Once they hit the city, it was almost ten forty-five. Everyone was checking their weapons. Benson gave Shepard an earpiece in case they got lost. They were standing in front of the club, and they could see two of the bouncers smoking. One in normal human form and the other in vampire form.

Daniel rolled down his window to see if the others were with them, and they were still flying up in the sky. *"Arnold, are your people ready?"* Benson yelled at him.

"Yes. Waiting for your signal!" He told Daniel.

"Okay Dock. Ready? Let us do this in three. One, two, THREE!"

Dock then took off at high speed at the alleyway heading to the front of the club. When Dock turned on the headlights it was too late for the bouncers to move.

BOOM

He hit them both, slamming into The Nipple Clamps club.

Once the three of them got out of the car, every Lycan and every Dhampir followed right behind them. More minion vampires came out from the club to fight. Benson and Shepard were shooting at everything coming their way, while Dock and the Lycans were ripping off body parts. Daniel and Ally were making their way upstairs to the office hoping to find Koi and Rebekah. They were stopped by another bouncer and this one was huge, he had big muscles. Nothing was going to work on this big motherfucker.

Benson reached behind his back to retrieve his sword but was interrupted by a tap on his back. Benson turned around to see Arnold standing behind him.

"1935, let me deal with this one. I must fight this... how do you say... big hole of ass?" He asked Benson.

Shepard and Benson moved out of the way for Arnold.

"By the way, it's big asshole!" He told Arnold.

Arnold nodded and began fighting.

Benson and Ally made it to the office. Daniel checked the door to see if it was unlocked, but it wasn't. Benson kicked the door open and there were a few vampires waiting for him and Shepard on the other side. They blew and chopped them away, killing them all easily. The office was now empty. They checked to see if there was a secret door.

Benson looked at the vampires on the ground. They all turned to ash at the same time. Once the ash cleared enough for Benson to see, he saw one still lying on the floor. Benson was relieved. He grabbed him by the neck, *"Hey fuckface! Where did they go?"* He asked the vampire.

The vampire replied with his last breath, *"There is a button on the bookcase. Just keep searching the bi..."* the vampire turned to dust before he could finish.

Benson and Ally went to the bookshelf. Ally suggested they just go through every book. Benson's solution was to knock over the books till one doesn't knock down. So they went that route. They knocked down all the books till one stayed.

Benson looked at the title and it was the bible. *"Really? You fucking assholes! That is so wrong."* He mumbled under his breath.

He pulled the book out towards him, and the wall opened revealing stairs going down.

Before they could go down, he turned to Shepard and said, *"It's best if I go alone. You have no idea what could happen. Get everyone and let them know we found a hidden passage. Go now!"*

She did what Benson asked her to do and left him alone. Benson got his shotgun from his shoulder and started to head down. Candles lit up the walls throughout the passageway. He killed a few vampires along the way down. He could hear chatting getting louder. It meant he was getting closer. He saw Koi and Rebekah talking to Amaya. She was tied up from a makeshift cross and she was in a white cloth. Koi and Rebekah were in their black robes along with a few vampires. Rebekah had the drug V in her hand. They were going to give it to Amaya.

Benson came out of the shadows with his shotgun loaded right before Rebekah could give her the drug. Benson shot her hand clean off. And when the minions noticed they were attacking Benson. Daniel shot them one at a time when he ran out of shells, he used his sword to slice and dice them one at a time. The more he killed the more there were. Then finally hopefully he got the last one Koi and Rebekah were nowhere to be seen. Just as Daniel was about to untie Amaya, he felt a sharp pain in his head, and he went down like a sack of marbles. When he turned around it was Rebekah holding the doll of Benson as she had a big needle in his head, Koi came over and started kicking Benson in the ribs.

"You're not so bad now, are you? What do you have to say for yourself?" He asked him.

"Are you a top or bottom? Or does Rebekah even know you go both ways?" He asked Koi.

Rebekah, with her what used to be her stubby hand grew back, still holding the doll, let's go of the needle in Benson's head. She looked confused at Koi and asked him, *"Lover, what is he talking about? You know I'm the only one who can go both ways."*

"I don't know what he is talking about!" Koi laughed nervously. *"He is talking crazy. You know how I like to watch you go down on girls while I jackoff."*

"Please! I saw a guy go down on you and from the look on your face, you enjoyed every second of it."

"He's goddamn lying. I never liked it. You're the best at giving me head baby! Please! Can we just end this? Kill him. Put that needle in his heart so we can tell Drake that it's done." Koi pleaded with Rebekah.

Daniel was getting up from the ground and he told Rebekah, *"Shit! Drake knows. He saw it with his own eyes."*

Then she dropped the voodoo doll of Daniel. She was going to leave but Koi stopped her. *"Wait! Babe wait and listen. I have to tell you something. Please turn around."* He pleaded with Rebekah.

She turned around to look at Koi, he then confessed to her, *"I never loved you. I just wanted to do business for myself. Benson is right. I do go both ways."* Koi grabbed Benson's sword and aimed it at Rebekah's heart. Before Rebekah could process what was happening, it was too late. She died instantly.

Koi pulls the knife out of Rebekah and her body falls to the ground. Koi throws the sword away from Daniel and Rebekah's body and pulls out a gun, pointing it at Daniel. *"You fuck. You are fucking stupid half human shit head. I think I should kill you in front of this witch bitch! Speaking of which, I knew you were undercover! Sacred Fire is next on my list, right after I kill off this fucker and the rest of the Invictus Society. I'm in love with Dr. Drake. I find him so handsome and good looking. That night when he got mad at me, I was still hard, and it made my nipples hard. I'm so glad his blood is turning your parasite humans into our slaves."* He told Benson.

Just then, more minion vampires were coming inside. Benson still had his hands up with the gun still pointing at his face. He looked at Amaya thinking this was it. He will never see his daughter or Amaya again.

Then BOOM! The gun Koi was holding was gone. Benson turned to see who it was. It was Ally. She shot the gun Koi was holding. The minions were now focused on Shepard, but she had backup behind her. It was the Dhampirs and the Lycans ready to battle and so was Ally. Koi took off running like a little bitch while Daniel went to untie Amaya.

After he untied her, she hugged and kissed him. *"Are you okay?"* He asked her.

"Yes, go get that fruitcake!" She told him.

As Benson was leaving, he gave Amaya his coat to cover up and his hat, along with his sword. He had no weapons or bullets left. Just the golden dagger that was hiding behind his back. He stopped and pulled it out from his back and went after Koi. Everyone else continued fighting.

After a few minutes Benson lost track of Koi. *"Come on out you half of a fruitcake. Come out and fight me like a man and not like a pussy!"* He told Koi.

It was dark in that part of the underground cave, but he could hear Koi moving around. Then he heard the sound of a sword. His Dhampir senses kicked in and Benson moved out of the way just in time. Behind him, Koi who had yellowish eyes now and his fangs were longer was a lot uglier than before. when the sword made a big spark when Daniel moved out of the way.

"Well, you look like my ex when she's on crystal meth." He insulted Koi.

"Once I'm done with you. I'm gonna fuck you in the ass and make you like it." He told Benson.

"Nah. No thanks. I rather keep my ass cheeks unharmed. I don't wanna know where you got that sword." He told Koi.

Then with a snap of a finger, Koi lit up the candles, lighting up the underground cave so they could fight better.

They both went right to left and left to right seeing who was gonna make the first move.

Daniel went first, he used the dagger to see if can stab him, but Koi was quick. *"Well at least you're quick. Not like the last God. He was on too much cocaine. I had to kill him like twenty times in the 1980s. The 80s were a bad one for me Koi. You try killing a God vampire all coked up on cocaine and blood. The hair and dress styles were awesome, and they had some badass music."* He told Koi.

"Shut the fuck up and fight. Make your move again." He told Benson.

Again, Benson tried the same move, but this time Koi moved. He tried a different move, Koi moved again but he got Benson right in the back. Daniel went down on his knees. He tried to get up, but he couldn't because of the blood loss. His powers that were lost from Rebekah's Voodoo doll weren't back yet.

Just then, Koi saw the golden dagger Benson was holding. Koi grabbed it from him and threw it towards the rocks on the bottom of the cave.

Benson had to crawl into the darkness to recover.

"Give up old man. Just give up. Let us win and rule the world. I promise I will take care of your daughter and that bitch you fucked. I will fuck them both over your dead body." Koi laughed demonically.

Out of nowhere, something inside Benson made him snap. His body began to transform into something different. He grew taller and his muscles were bigger than before. His teeth were sharper, and his ears pointed out more. His eyes were fire red.

Koi didn't see Benson's transformation. He only heard Benson cry out in pain which made him laugh even more. *"Ah! What's the matter? Did I hit a nerve? How about this Benson? I know about your dead wife. How about I dig up her body and fuck her rotting corpse as well? Come on and get up and keep fighting!"* Koi continued to laugh.

Chapter Twenty

"*KOI, YOU JUST PISSED ME THE FUCK OFF! DON'T YOU EVER TALK ABOUT MY DAUGHTER, MY DEAD WIFE, OR AMAYA!*" Benson yelled in a demonic voice. Then Daniel came out from the dark and he was transformed into a demonic creature complete with wings that expanded thirty feet wide.

The look on Koi's face went from shocked to worry, but then it went to cocky. *"Oh, I can play this game too watch,"* said Koi.

Just then he transformed into the same thing. Koi flew up in the air and so did Benson. They began fighting, clawing at each other, punching each other, and biting each other. Hitting each other on the big rocks. Koi almost killed Daniel with a sharp Rock that was hanging from the top of the cave. Benson punched him and they both missed it.

With one last effort Koi took Benson and was about to shove him down to the bottom where the sharp rocks were. Daniel saw what was coming. He did one final move to get out of the way and kill Koi. He kneed him in the balls. With that move, Koi let's go of Benson to cover them up and started to rub them.

Daniel flew behind Koi, grabbed his wings, and started to rip them off with his feet. Benson kicked Koi hard to the bottom of the sharp pointy rocks, killing Koi instantly. Daniel was feeling the power wearing off, so he went back to the ground. He could see Amaya, Ally, Dock, and Arnold. The rest were coming to see him. Everyone saw Benson's true form, even Arnold was shocked.

"He is the prophecy one. Shit holy!" Replied Arnold.

Benson went back to his normal form, and he went to Arnold and added, *"It's holy shit."*

"What the fuck?" Amaya was still in shock.

Benson was still catching a breather. *"Your grandma Martha was right all along. I'm special. Wait! what time is it?"*

"It's eleven forty-five," Ally told him after looking at her watch.

"Shit! I have to go. The Invictus Society are gonna kill Leah!" He told them.

"You're never gonna make it in time." Amaya told him.

He just grinned and said, *"Watch me!"*

He asked Amaya for his sword back and she threw it at him. He caught it. With his powers back, he started to run fast. He never ran so fast in his life. He didn't have a watch or phone on him, so he didn't know the time once he got there. Dead bodyguards were everywhere. Expecting trouble, he took out his sword just in case. He took the elevator down to the medical to see if he could stop them from pulling the plug on Leah. He found nothing but dead bodies that lead to Leah's room.

"Shit, I hope I'm not too late!" He told himself, and he went into his daughter's room.

He found more bodies, but his daughter was still alive. He turned over the bodies one by one. April, Gina, Andrea, and Carla were still alive, just knocked out. The only bodies that were dead were some bodyguards and the boss who was still holding a knife. Then he went to see Leah. She was still in a coma. Daniel rubbed her hair and kissed her forehead and grinned. When Daniel turned around, he was grabbed by the neck by none other than Akasha.

"You fucking big bitch! Let me go so I can kill you!" Benson said as he struggled to get out of her grip. Her grip was so powerful and strong that he had to let go of his sword to use both of his hands to get a hold of Akasha's wrist.

"I don't think so my dear Dhampir. You see, it is almost midnight, and my ritual is almost complete. I just need one more ounce of blood. I figured I can use yours to become whole again. oh, my darling Robert please come here." She said.

Out of the darkness comes Robert. He looked like he had not slept in days. He was wearing the same outfit when he escaped Benson and the police.

"Yes, my queen? My Love." He told her.

"Be a dear and get those scissors and scalpel." She replied.

"Yes, my love. Once we do this, you promise to be mine forever?' Robert asked her.

"Yes, stop asking me that! Now do what I say!" She angrily told him.

He left to fetch the scissors and scalpel, while Akasha put Benson high on the wall holding one arm out while she choked him out.

Herrera returned with the scissors and scalpel.

"Now get a ladder. And impale his hands." She told him.

He did what he was told once again. He put three scissors into Benson's hand using the butt of his gun to do it.

"Now the other one." She told him.

He did the same thing and then she let go of his neck. He was hanging there with both arms laid across from him. Then she got the scalpel from Robert. She got close to Benson's wrist and started to cut it to get his blood. Blood came running from his wrist and she started to suck and drink the blood.

By the time she was done, the clock rang midnight. It was Halloween. Leah woke up from her comatose state. Benson was shocked that his daughter finally woke up. Little did he know it wasn't his daughter. Leah got out of her bed and went straight to Akasha hugging her.

"You fucking big cunt bitch. I'm gonna get you and blast your ass into pieces!" Benson threatened Akasha as he slowly bled out.

"Ha, you fool! My powers are back. I'm stronger than ever and what did you call me? Ah yes, the mega bitch is back, and when I find my love, the three of us will rule the world." She confessed to Benson.

"Yeah, you heard that right Daniel. I'm gonna be king of the world," announced Herrera.

"Oh, I'm sorry my love. I wasn't talking about you. I was talking about my long-lost true husband, Justin Drake, or I like to call him Dracula. Thank you for freeing me and killing those women for me, but you're not what I'm looking for. I'd rather fuck a small cock old man than you, but for your rewards you get this." Akasha told Robert as she snapped her fingers.

"Robert! Watch out!" Benson yelled to his friend.

By the time Robert figured it out it was too late. A hand came out of his chest ripping out his heart and killing him instantly.

Daniel couldn't do anything but watch Robert die. Robert's dead body fell to the ground and the person who killed him was revealed. Daniels face went pale. He knew who this man was. He saw him a lot in his nightmares. It was none other than Drake. Also known as Dracula.

"You? Was it always you? But why?" He asked Dracula.

Dracula was about six feet ten, black, and muscles with a goatee.

"You see Dhampir, you did my dirty work for me. For years you killed off the Gods of Vampires. I knew you were a Dhampir since you were a baby. I sensed it and once you grew up, I had to come out of hiding. I knew you were gonna find my love Akasha. But then you turned her into stone. I lost the signal. Once she got your friend here to do her work, I had to come out of hiding again. That is why I let Koi and Rebekah sell my blood to turn these filthy humans into my minions. They will serve us." He told Benson with his British accent. *"And now, in the new year. When my blood hits the universe everyone will serve us. But don't worry about your daughter Daniel. If you survive this and I hope you do, I will make sure I will tie you up while Akasha cuts your eyelids open, and I fuck her in front of you. And then when I'm done with her, I'll make sure she will kill you. Funny, you just need a crown of thorns to finish off your crucifixion."* He told Benson.

Daniel struggled to get loose. He wanted to kill Dracula more than ever for threatening his daughter.

Dracula yelled at the top of his lungs and replied, *"I WILL MAKE THEM FEEL MY PAIN!"* Thunder roared and lightning flashed outside the window.

"I will make sure they will never ever have to feel your pain." Benson whispered.

"Look. More blood is coming out of you. You will bleed out slowly." He taunted Benson. *"I have an idea come here dear."* Dracula points to Leah.

Leah does what she is told. He picks up Benson's sword with his superpowers. The steel doesn't burn him at all. He noticed the names of the Gods of Vampires on it crossed out on the sword. He turned and gave it to Leah. *"Now dear, I want you to cut his throat so he can bleed out faster. You got that? His throat under his chin."*

Dracula showed Leah where to cut. He picked up Leah because Daniel was high on the wall. She and Daniel both locked eyes for the first time since she was a little girl, and he noticed how Leah had Rebecca's green eyes.

"Leah, don't I love y..." Benson began to say but it was too late.

Without hesitation, Leah slit Benson's throat. Bleeding him out faster.

Once he stopped moving, Dracula checked to see what Benson had under his shirt. It was Benson's wedding ring and the Medallion. He ripped it off the chain from around his neck. He put Benson's wedding ring on his left ring finger, then he just dropped the medallion on the ground.

Dracula looked at Benson whose head was down. Daniel slowly looked up and they locked eyes. He said to Benson, *"Pitiful to think, after all the trouble you gave me, that you'd go down so easily. The others may be out there, but it's quite a treat to see you fall so painfully right before me. At least now, you are out of my way for good. Sleep now hero, you've failed the humans more than enough. I'll take care of them and your daughter in your stead.''* He crossed Benson's feet together. Dracula admired Daniel. He had done an evil smile and then he laughed. After that he took Daniel's sword as an award.

Dracula, Akasha, and Leah left the Invictus Society building together. Once they were outside the building, the weather finally cleared, and they disappeared into the night holding hands.

To Be Continued...
In Dead Rites Part 3.
Final Rites
Coming Soon

Acknowledgements

First, I want to thank God for blessing me every day.

Then, I would like to acknowledge My Dad Willie, my sister Valorie, my Brother Willie Ben, My Sister-in-law Misty, My Bother in law Joey, My uncle Pete, My aunt Sylvia, My Nieces, and Nephews.

Next, I want to acknowledge. Deedra R, Pilar S, Robert H, Martha K, Andrea L, Mariah E, Rayne W, April T, Ally Y, Carla M, Trina M, Thomas S. Christina K. Francine D. and of course, my fur daughter Harley. If I forgot anyone, I do apologize. Thank you for your support and for keeping me going and I hope I continue to make you proud. Your inspiration has gotten me this far! I love you all.

Next, I want to acknowledge my editor, Felicia Witte. again, without you my books wouldn't be here.

Professor Nadie D, you're the shit.

D2D thank you for publishing my books.

For the Dead Rite readers, I hope you have enjoyed part two of this series. I hope you are ready for part 3.

And finally, I want to acknowledge someone special near and dear to my heart and that is my goddaughter Lorelei S. I love you sweet pea.

182

Don't miss out!

Visit the website below and you can sign up to receive emails whenever Markus Danielson publishes a new book. There's no charge and no obligation.

https://books2read.com/r/B-A-XGHZ-MODXD

BOOKS2READ

Connecting independent readers to independent writers.

Did you love *Blood Rites*? Then you should read *Dead Rites*[1] by Markus Danielson!

[2]

In 1935, a New York private detective Daniel Benson, is down on his luck after losing his family due to his alcholism. He has made it a goal to win his family back but he needs one good case to get the money.

When all hope is about to be lost a client walks in with a job Benson can't refuse. Benson is more than ever ready to get started on his new case but it won't be easy.

As he starts to uncover secrets of his clients, he starts to uncover secrets about himself as well.

---

1. https://books2read.com/u/mZXvrE

2. https://books2read.com/u/mZXvrE

The more he uncovers the more people die. Will Benson give up or will he solve the most complicated case he has ever endured?

Also by Markus Danielson

Dead Rites Series
Blood Rites
Dead Rites

About the Author

Markus Danielson has found his true calling and passion. He enjoys writing short stories, and poems. Markus Danielson was born and raised in Colorado. Whenever he is not writing, you can catch him playing video games, hanging out with family and friends, Or playing with his dog Harley. He is a collector of Batman collectibles. As well a huge Colorado sports fan, but also a huge wrestling fan.